Discover the DARK ENCHANTMENT series

DARK ENCHANTMENT

Firespell

LOUISE COOPER

DARK ENCHANTMENT

The Lost Brides

THERESA RADCLIFFE

DARK ENCHANTMENT

The Hounds of Winter

LOUISE COOPER

DARK ENCHANTMENT

DARK ENCHANTMENT

House of Thorns

JUDY DELAGHTY

DARK ENCHANTMENT

Valley of Wolves

THERESA RADCLIFFE

Other titles in the DARK ENCHANTMENT series

Blood Dance

LOUISE COOPER

PUFFIN BOOKS

PUFFIN BOOKS

Published by the Penguin Group
Penguin Books Ltd, 27 Wrights Lane, London W8 5TZ, England
Penguin Books USA Inc., 375 Hudson Street, New York, New York 10014, USA
Penguin Books Australia Ltd, Ringwood, Victoria, Australia
Penguin Books Canada Ltd, 10 Alcorn Avenue, Toronto, Ontario, Canada M4V 3B2
Penguin Books (NZ) Ltd, 182–190 Wairau Road, Auckland 10, New Zealand

Penguin Books Ltd, Registered Offices: Harmondsworth, Middlesex, England

First published 1996
1 3 5 7 9 10 8 6 4 2

Set in 12/14 pt Sabon Monotype
Typeset by Datix International Limited, Bungay, Suffolk

Made and printed in England by Clays Ltd, St Ives plc

CHAPTER I

I N HER DREAM Garland was two years old again, and very frightened.

Somehow, she knew she was dreaming. But in a way that only made matters worse, for the strangeness of being very small gave the nightmare an even more chilling edge. And something about it was frighteningly, horribly *real*. Almost as if it had all happened before . . .

In the dream it was night. Garland had woken suddenly, to hear a strange sound outside in the darkness of the forest beyond her house. She had begun to cry, and almost at once her mother came hurrying in. But though she hugged Garland and soothed her, Garland knew something was wrong. And now, by the unsteady light of one candle that cast menacing shadows on the ceiling, Garland huddled, trembling, in her mother's arms, listening as the sound out there in the night grew louder and closer. She had never heard such a sound before and hoped with all her heart that she would never have to hear it again. A rhythmic *thud . . . thud . . . thud* as something she couldn't name and couldn't imagine moved slowly, grimly past the house along the forest track. It sounded almost like men marching. But Garland knew in her bones that it was not. Whatever stirred out there in the night was something far stranger, and as she turned her head fearfully towards the curtained window of her bedroom she heard her mother's voice say softly and quickly:

'There's no need to be afraid, little one. They won't hurt us. But we must not look out of the window tonight. Whatever we do, we must not look outside!'

Thud . . . thud . . . thud . . . The sounds continued, each one driving a new arrow of terror into Garland's heart. The candle flame wavered, and the shadows on the ceiling seemed to quake in time with the awful, steady marching rhythm. Then suddenly the candle-light flared, brightened, seemed to fill the room –

And she woke to the first, pale light of a summer dawn.

Garland sat up in bed, shivering as the last tatters of the dream fled from her mind. *That nightmare again.* She *had* had it before. In fact it had haunted her for thirteen years, and every time it was exactly the same. The dim room, the eerie sounds, her mother's words of warning . . . it had all seemed so real. And, as she had done many times before, Garland asked herself if perhaps it was. Had the events of her dream actually happened to her when she was very small? She would have been too young to remember such a thing clearly. But was she reliving an episode from her own past?

She could have asked her mother, of course. But somehow she had never quite plucked up the courage. Once, a year or so ago, she had tried to drop hints about the dream, hoping that her questions might be answered. But her mother had brushed her hesitant words aside, saying quickly that dreams were harmless and meaningless and Garland shouldn't worry herself over nothing. She had then firmly changed the subject. As if, or so it seemed to Garland, she wanted to pretend that the matter had never been raised.

Garland frowned at that thought, then abruptly pushed it away. Her room was shadowy; she wanted suddenly to banish the shadows, for they reminded her too much of the dream. So, slipping out of bed, she ran to her window to pull back the curtains and look out at the day. The forest was dense and the trees encroached almost to the garden wall. But this morning even their dark gloominess couldn't bring a chilly little tingle to her skin as it usually did. For above the trees the sky was starting to turn from the watery gold of sunrise to a bright, clear blue. There wasn't a cloud to be seen; the world looked bright and fresh, and as she looked at the scene the last of Garland's unease faded away and she smiled. She wasn't going to let any nightmare spoil her joy this morning. For today was a great milestone in her life. More than that; it was the *happiest* day of her life. For this was the day when she would officially become betrothed to Coryn.

Her thoughts seemed to take wing then, and fly to the grander, older house, three miles away on the far side of the forest, where Coryn lived with his widowed mother. Garland and Coryn had known each other since they were children, and from the very beginning Garland had fallen in love with the tall, blond-haired boy with his quiet blue eyes and gentle smile. Coryn wasn't like the other boys of the farms and villages in the district. Where they enjoyed fighting and horseplay, he loved music and books. And dancing. That, Garland reflected, was what had truly brought them together, for dancing was one of her own greatest pleasures. Then, when she was thirteen and Coryn fifteen, they had partnered each other at the Harvest Fair and her secret dream had come true. For, when the first dance ended, Coryn had held on to her hands and, gazing into her eyes, had told her that he loved her.

Garland would remember for ever just how he had looked in that memorable moment. So solemn, so serious – and so afraid that she might scorn him, or even laugh at him. And she remembered, too, how his look of uncertainty had changed to a look of joy as she shyly told him that there could never be anyone else for her.

Two years had passed since that momentous

evening. In that time, their love had grown stronger – and now a final crown was about to be set on Garland's happiness. Her parents and Coryn's mother had agreed to a match between their children. And tonight, at Coryn's house, a great party would take place to celebrate their betrothal.

They wouldn't marry for several years, of course, for they were both too young. But Garland was content to wait. She would wear a silver ring on her finger, Coryn's betrothal gift, and the world would know that they belonged to each other. And when a few years had passed and they *were* married, then a whole new life would begin for them both. They would be so happy. They would –

'Garland!' Her mother's voice called suddenly from downstairs. 'Garland, are you awake?'

Garland snapped out of her daydream. 'Yes, Mother!' she called back.

'Then hurry and dress yourself, child. Breakfast will be early today; there's a great deal to do.'

The gown she would wear tonight was laid on a chair. Blue brocade – the blue of Coryn's eyes – and stitched with pearls that were starting to shine as the sunlight through her window grew stronger. Garland felt a joyous urge to try it on just one more time, but quelled the impulse. Only a few more hours, and evening would come. She had waited two years for this. She could contain her impatience for a little while longer.

Her heart soared, and she sang a lilting, dancing song as she hurried to her wardrobe to find more sober clothes for the day ahead.

CHAPTER II

IN THE EARLY light of the morning Coryn's mother was in the garden, picking what flowers she could find among the tangled and overgrown wilderness. Behind her the house rose grey and gloomy; the sun hadn't touched it yet and its shadow seemed to put an unnatural chill on the day.

She was unaware that anyone was watching her until, suddenly, a voice spoke out of the dawn.

'Where is your son, widow?'

Coryn's mother turned with a start. At the edge of the garden stood an ancient crone. She had deathly pale skin, and her white hair hung down in two long braids over a worn dress patched with motley colours. The widow stared at her, and fear crept slowly into her eyes. For she recognized what the crone was.

She said, in a voice that quavered just a little, 'Have we met before, old mother?'

'No,' the crone replied. 'But I know who you are, and I know your story. And I ask you again: where is your son?'

The widow licked her dry lips. 'Coryn was away early. He was gone into the forest, to find branches to decorate the house.'

'Ah, yes; for the party to celebrate his betrothal. I hear it is to take place tonight. Is this true?'

Coryn's mother wanted to deny it, but as she met the faded yet unnervingly steady gaze, she knew she couldn't lie. 'Yes,' she whispered. 'It is true.'

The crone nodded. 'And have you warned him?' she asked. 'Have you told him what may lie in his future?'

The widow's hands began to shake. 'You . . . know about that?'

'About the bane that has shadowed your family through so many generations? Yes; for the knowledge came to me in a dream. But I see now, from the fear in your eyes, that your son is still unaware of the truth.' Suddenly her gaze became very intent. 'If you love him, widow, you must tell him now. It is your duty, as it has been the duty of so many mothers before you. He has a right to know.'

For a few seconds Coryn's mother was silent. Then suddenly, desperately, she burst out, 'How can I bring myself to reveal such a thing to him? It is too cruel!'

'Cruel or not, it must be done.'

Tears began to trickle down the widow's cheeks and her voice dropped to a whisper. 'If I could just wait a while longer . . . Coryn is so happy, and it will break my heart to shatter his joy. In a year or two, perhaps . . .'

But the crone shook her head. 'No. My dream has told me that this is the proper time.' She looked into the widow's eyes again, and there was a strange, deep pity in her expression. 'Fate cannot be defied, and if the Nine should claim their fee, it must be paid. Tell your son, widow. Warn him. In your heart, you know you have no other choice.'

Coryn's mother turned away, covering her face with her hands. She tried to think of another argument, something, *anything*, that would deny the truth of what the crone had said. But the words would not come. At last she raised her head to plead one final time.

But where the crone had stood, there was only an empty space.

The widow stared towards the forest. How had the old woman left so silently? There was no trace of her to be seen; not a blade of flattened grass, not the smallest movement among the leaves of the trees. Had she really been there at all, or was she a ghost, a dream? The widow could not tell. But deep inside herself she knew that she could not ignore what had happened. Dream or reality, the crone was right. She must tell the truth at long last.

The sound of hoofs on the forest track alerted her then, and she turned to see Coryn on his bay mare emerging from the trees. He was smiling as he called out to her, and a great sheaf of green leaves was laid before him over the saddle. He looked so happy . . . the widow's heart seemed to turn to lead as she went to meet him.

Coryn looked at her face and frowned, puzzled. 'What is it, Mother? Is something wrong?' He slid down from the mare's back and tried to take her hand, but she drew it out of his reach.

'Coryn,' she said gently, 'Coryn, my dear son, come into the house.' She paused. 'There is something I must tell you. I should have done it a long time ago, but . . . I didn't have the courage. Now though . . . now, it cannot wait any longer. You must know the truth about our family – and about yourself.'

Two hours later, Coryn emerged from the house, unhitched his mare once more and rode her away into the forest. His face was a dead-white mask, and he did not once look back at the house, but spurred the mare on until he reached a place where the trees gave way to open grassland. Before him a hill rose, its bulk dark and menacing even under the sun's brilliant light. And on the crown of the hill were strange shapes . . .

Coryn tethered the mare to a tree and began to climb the hill. As he climbed, the wind blew sharp against his face and whipped his hair across his eyes. Its soughing seemed to mock him as he drew nearer to the top. And there on the summit he stopped and stared, with hurt and angry eyes, at the great slabs of stone that formed a circle on the hilltop.

'*Why?*' He whispered the word, and the wind threw it back to him like a mournful echo. '*What harm did we do to you, to make you exact a revenge like this?*'

His only answer was the bark of a dog far away in the distance. The stones stood unmoving, lifeless, aloof. Yet he felt the power of them, a cold, ancient power that defied the beautiful day and sent a chill through to the marrow of his bones. And he knew that, if the power chose to awake, he could not hope to stand against it.

He looked up at the sky. But there was nothing for him there; only a hard, remote blueness in which the sun blazed, indifferent to his misery. Coryn knew he must return to the house. There was no choice. He had to prepare for the day ahead, and the evening that would follow, and he had to pretend that all was well and nothing had changed. But it had changed. It *had*. And Coryn didn't know if he had the inner strength to face it.

He turned, and with shoulders slumping and eyes dull with despair, began slowly to descend the hill to his waiting horse.

Garland and her parents set out for Coryn's home an hour before sunset; her father and mother on their bay horses and Garland on her dapple-grey pony. For a mile or so they rode among the trees, then for another mile they crossed a patch of open grassland before the forest began again. And on the grassland, Garland's eyes were drawn uneasily towards the Nine Men.

The Nine Men formed the oldest landmark in the district. A circle of nine great stones at the top of a grassy hill, each one standing half again as tall as a man. No one knew when or why they had come to be there, or how they had got their strange name; their origins were steeped in mystery. But for more time than anyone could count – or possibly even imagine – they had stood on the hilltop, like sentinels against the skyline, grey and forbidding. For many generations it had been a tradition for the people of the nearby villages to gather at the circle for festivals and celebrations, and Garland had attended many such revels with her parents. But for all the merriment that took place there, the hilltop still had an eerie atmosphere. The stones were held in awe; almost in dread. And sometimes the older villagers left offerings of bread or flowers at the circle, to appease what they darkly and reverently called the 'spirits of the stones'.

As Garland looked at the brooding shapes she felt a chill shiver go through her despite the summer evening warmth. From the attic rooms of Coryn's house the distant outline of this hill was just visible, and Coryn had once said that the Nine Men could, if they chose, watch the house by day and night. He had laughed as he said it, but his laughter had had an uneasy edge. When they were married, Garland too would live under the stones' frowning gaze. And it was not a prospect that she relished.

'Garland,' said her mother suddenly, 'you're dawdling! Come along – anyone would think you were reluctant to go to your own betrothal celebration!'

Garland snapped out of her daydream. Her mother was watching her, eyebrows raised; a little way ahead her father looked back with a grin, and winked. She pushed the Nine Men from her mind, shook her pony's reins to hurry it along, and they continued on their way.

But as they rode, the rhythmic thud of the horses' hoofs in the grass reminded her, suddenly and unnervingly, of the sounds she had heard in her dream . . .

CHAPTER III

THE HOUSE WHERE Coryn and his mother lived stood near the edge of the forest, and was built of grey stone with tall chimneys and many gables. Years ago, Garland knew, Coryn's family had held glittering parties and dances in the house's great ballroom, and as she rode up to the imposing front door it was easy to imagine the building ablaze with light as yet another splendid revel began. But as time passed, those happy days had been eclipsed by misfortune. Many heads of the household had died young, including Coryn's own father, whom Coryn could barely remember. The bereaved widows had struggled on to bring up their children alone, but money had dwindled and life became harder for each generation. Now, the house had an air of neglect that made it seem cold and unwelcoming. The garden was a tangle, the old stones shabby, and the wonderful ballroom was in such disrepair that it could no longer be used. It was kept locked, and Garland had never so much as peeked inside. But from Coryn's description she could imagine how magnificent it had once been, with its tall, shimmering windows, myriad candles and – most imposing of all – the exquisitely carved wooden pillars that formed a circle around the edge of the great room. Now though, so Coryn said, the windows were dulled and grimy, the candle-sconces stood empty and the pillars and floor were full of woodworm. All that was left to recall what the ballroom had once been were an old spinet gathering dust in a corner, and, above the door into the ballroom, a wooden frieze carved with the family motto: '*Dance the dance and step the measure*'.

Garland had seen the frieze for herself, and was greatly intrigued by that motto. Its meaning puzzled her, but it seemed wonderfully apt for herself and Coryn, with their love of dancing. Yet when she asked Coryn's mother where the motto had come from, the widow could tell her very little. All she knew, she said, was that it had been adopted by the family many, many generations ago. Perhaps, she added a little sadly, it dated from more prosperous days, when the ballroom was in use and grand parties were still held. If so, then the motto was now all that remained to remind the family of those long-lost times.

Garland had asked no more questions, but in her mind she had made a small and secret promise to herself. The old days might be lost, but with her betrothal to Coryn, new days were about to begin. And those new days would bring hope to the old house again. When she and

Coryn were married, they could work together to restore the ballroom to its former glory. And in their happiness, the house would find a new lease of life.

So she arrived at the celebration feeling eager and joyful. But her joy did not last for long.

The celebrations began well enough. Coryn's mother was at the door to greet Garland with a kiss, and many neighbours had gathered to witness the betrothal ceremony and wish the young couple well. Coryn, however, was nowhere to be seen. He was upstairs, his mother said, getting ready, and would be down shortly. But as she spoke the words, a small frown crossed her face. Garland, suddenly anxious, was about to ask if something was wrong, when a movement on the landing above the entrance hall drew her attention. She looked up ... and saw Coryn coming slowly down the stairs.

Coryn looked as handsome as ever, tall and slim, his blond hair gleaming like silk. He was dressed elegantly in dark green velvet, he moved with easy grace – but as she looked at him, Garland knew instantly that something was terribly wrong.

'Garland.' To her astonishment he spoke her name not in his usual loving tone but strangely, almost coldly. When he reached the hall and came forward to kiss her, his lips were cold, too, and did not linger for more than the briefest of moments.

'Coryn . . .?' Garland tried to catch hold of his hand, but he evaded her grasp and moved a step away. Then, seeing that her parents were watching, he made an effort to cover his mood with a smile. But he was like an actor playing a part. He didn't *mean* it.

Baffled and dismayed, Garland strove to find a chance to ask Coryn what was wrong. But her attempts were in vain, for now they were among a crowd of people, the centre of attention, and it was impossible to snatch even one private moment. Perhaps, she told herself desperately, Coryn was simply nervous? Yes, yes; it *must* be that. There couldn't be any other reason for his strangeness. He hadn't changed his mind about her. Surely, *surely* he couldn't have changed his mind?

She was reassured when at last the betrothal ceremony began, for Coryn raised no objections but stood beside her and repeated the words that they had rehearsed together so many times. A promise that he loved her. A promise that they would one day be married. But he spoke so quietly that Garland could barely hear him, and as her parents and his mother gave their blessings she glanced uneasily up at him. His face was deadly pale, and the expression in his eyes was withdrawn, as if his thoughts were somewhere else entirely.

When the promises had been spoken, there was an awkward pause. Several seconds passed. Garland's father cleared his throat noisily. Then Coryn's mother said uneasily, 'Coryn . . . the ring . . .'

'Ah . . .' Coryn blinked and, reluctantly it seemed, brought the silver ring from his pocket. He didn't look at Garland, but took her hand and quickly, almost carelessly, slipped the ring on to her finger. When she tried to hold on to his hand he wouldn't allow it but pulled away. With that, the ceremony was done. They were betrothed. And Garland felt so miserable that she wanted to run out of the house, run to the garden, find a secret place to hide herself away and cry her heart out.

She couldn't do it, of course. No one else seemed to have realized that anything was wrong, and so she had to keep up a pretence of happiness. A feast was spread out on the table in the great hall, and the musicians hired for the evening were striking up for the first dance. Coryn led Garland out on to the floor, and for a few hopeful moments she thought that all would be well again. But it was not – for Coryn's heart was not in it. He danced beautifully, as he always did, but there was something stiff and unsettled in the way he moved. And he would not meet her gaze. His eyes were remote, his mouth unsmiling. It was as if he resented her, she thought. Or almost – almost – as if he *hated* her . . .

Once, during an interval in the dancing, the chance came to speak to Coryn alone. Garland caught hold of his hand, ignoring his quick attempt to evade her, and said, 'Coryn – Coryn, whatever's wrong?'

He turned his blue gaze on her at last, almost as if she were a stranger. 'Wrong?' he echoed. 'Nothing's wrong. Why should it be?'

'But it *is!*' Garland persisted. 'You've barely spoken a word to me all evening – you're cold and distant, and I don't understand! Oh, Coryn, what have I *done?*'

'Don't be silly,' Coryn said. 'You're imagining things.' And with that he turned and walked away.

Garland stared at his departing back, feeling helpless and bewildered. Every instinct she possessed urged her to run after him and *make* him tell her why he was behaving in this way. But Coryn was talking to a neighbour now. She couldn't confront him without causing an embarrassing scene, and he must know that. He was deliberately making it impossible for them to be alone together.

Miserably, Garland looked at the ring on her finger. It had meant everything to her, yet now it seemed to be worth nothing. If she tore it off, if she threw it across the room and renounced the vows she had just made, would Coryn care? It seemed not. But why? *Why?* She had no answers.

The rest of the evening was an ordeal for Garland. But at last it ended. The guests departed, offering congratulations which she could hardly bear to hear, and then her own family's horses were brought to the door. Coryn didn't see them away but made an excuse and went back into the house. As she set off behind her father's bobbing lantern Garland looked back at the house, standing dark and solitary and cold in the night, and felt the tears she had been holding back start to pour down her cheeks. Her parents wouldn't see her crying in the dark. She didn't want them to see. She didn't want anyone to know how desolate she was. She wanted time to be alone.

To *think* . . .

Coryn's mother watched until the three horses were out of sight, then closed the front door very quietly, and went in search of her son.

Coryn was in the dining hall. He was standing by the table, looking down at the remains of the feast, and in the candle-light his face was strained. His mother watched him for a few moments, then said,

'Coryn. You behaved very cruelly tonight.'

Coryn looked up quickly. 'Cruelly?'

'Yes. Don't pretend you don't know what I mean.' Now the widow's voice grew angry. 'How *could* you treat poor Garland in such a way? She was in tears when they left!'

'Yes,' said Coryn. 'I know.'

'To watch you with her, anyone would think that you no longer loved her!'

There was a long pause. Then Coryn sighed, the sound seeming to echo strangely in the spacious room.

'Mother,' he said, 'you of all people know how much I love Garland.' Suddenly his expression became terribly bitter, and he looked at her with pain in his eyes. 'But however much I love her, I know that we can have no future together!'

'Coryn –'

'No.' He held up a hand, silencing her. 'Don't pretend, Mother. It's too late, for now you've told me the truth. There *is* no future for me. I'll die young, just as my father and grandfather did, and many more before them. It's my destiny – and I can't escape it!'

The widow's lips began to tremble and she clasped her hands tightly together. In a small voice she said, 'My son . . . it might not happen. The sign might not come for another twenty or thirty years. It might never come again!'

But Coryn only laughed hollowly. 'Oh, Mother, how many generations of our family have clung to that hope, only to have it dashed?' He crossed the room towards her and took hold of her hands in a grip that hurt. 'Remember what you said this morning? That you and Father had just five years of happiness. Long enough to have a son, and to start to hope that maybe there was a chance for your future. But then, when I was three, harvest time came round again. When the harvest moon rose, it was red. It was the sign you had dreaded. And within one more day, *they* had claimed another victim, and Father was dead.'

The widow began to sob, very softly. Coryn continued, 'I've thought about it, Mother. All through today. I don't want Garland to suffer as you did. I don't want her to be left a broken-hearted young widow, as you were. *That* would be far crueller than anything I did this evening!'

His mother pulled away from him and wiped her eyes. 'But,' she said, 'isn't it the worst cruelty of all to treat her in this way when she can't be told the reason?'

Coryn sighed again and walked to the window. The summer night was clear, the sky above the encroaching trees filled with stars. In the distance, he knew, the hill where the stone circle stood would be showing dark against the skyline. If he climbed to the top floor, he would see its brooding outline . . . Coryn shivered and said, 'What else can I do? The last thing I want in the world is to be unkind to Garland. And I do so much want to marry her. But, knowing what I know, how can I go on pretending that everything's normal? I can hardly bear to look at her.' He uttered a wretched little laugh. 'Who knows – maybe before long she will no longer want to marry me. She'll stop loving me. That would be for the best, wouldn't it?' The candles guttered suddenly, as though a cold, ghostly wind had blown into the room. Shadows stirred, and Coryn's eyes seemed to burn with an eerie sense of premonition . . . and of fear.

'Then, when I die,' he said, 'it will not break her heart. Above all else, I want to spare her that.'

CHAPTER IV

I N THE GLOW OF the moonlight streaming through her window that night, Garland lay tossing and turning in bed. Memories of the terrible evening plagued her like a waking nightmare, and over and over again, gnawing at her like a fever, was the question she couldn't answer. What had happened to Coryn, to make him behave the way he had?

Then, in the small hours, a terrible thought came to her. Was it possible that Coryn had fallen in love with another girl?

Garland sat bolt upright, staring into the black-and-silver gloom. What other reason could there be, she asked herself, for Coryn's sudden coldness towards her? Only days ago they had been so happy, but now he had changed utterly. Had he met someone else – someone he wanted to marry instead of Garland? It had been too late to stop the betrothal ceremony of course; Coryn couldn't break his promise without bringing her father's wrath down on his head. But did he now regret that promise?

A fresh wave of bitter misery washed over Garland and she lay down again, burying her face in her pillows and sobbing as though not only her heart but her soul would break in two. How, she asked herself, *how* could Fate be so cruel as to bring another girl into Coryn's life, to steal his love and make him betray all that they had been to each other? Garland was not good at hating, but she hated this unknown rival, whoever she might be, with all her power. And what made her angrier still was the feeling that there was nothing, nothing in the world that she could do to win Coryn back to her!

Garland finally cried herself to sleep. Terrible dreams haunted her, dreams of love and loss and yearning, and sometimes she called Coryn's name aloud, though no one else in the house was awake to hear her. But at last morning came. When she woke, the emotional storm had passed and her mind was clearer.

And she had a plan.

She had to know the truth about Coryn. For good or ill, she would rather know the worst than be plagued by doubts and fears. Coryn would tell her nothing; he had shown her that last night. So Garland resolved that she would begin to watch him, follow him in secret and find out where he went and whom he met. If she had a rival for his love, she would discover it soon enough.

She hated the idea of spying on the boy she adored, for it betrayed the trust she had always had in him and seemed somehow shabby. But then, hadn't Coryn betrayed *her* trust? She had to do it, Garland told herself. If she was ever to have any peace of mind, she had no other choice.

Garland set her plan in motion. It was easy enough to find excuses to leave the house without arousing awkward questions. A visit to the village market. A call on a friend. In high summer she had no lessons to study, so provided she was home each day before dark she was free to come and go as she pleased.

So every morning Garland saddled her pony and rode through the forest to a place at the edge of the trees, from where she could watch Coryn's house. And every day Coryn would appear, sometimes on horseback and sometimes on foot, and leave the house, never guessing that Garland was stealthily following and observing.

But what Garland saw, and what she learned, were not what she had expected and feared.

Coryn was not meeting another girl. In fact he was meeting no one at all, but instead was spending hours on end riding or walking alone in the forest. And, time after time, his wanderings took him to one place – the hill beyond the forest's edge, and the circle of stones known as the Nine Men.

From her hiding place among the trees, Garland gazed mystified as Coryn made his journeys to the hill. She couldn't begin to imagine what drew him to this strange and ancient place, but again and again he went there and spent many hours at the stone circle. Unlike some of the superstitious village people, he took no offerings for the Nine Men. He simply sat down at the edge of the ring, reading a book or, sometimes, writing. And occasionally he would get up and pace the perimeter of the circle, round and round, his head bowed as though he was deep in thought. Then as the sun began to wester he would return to his grazing horse, climb into the saddle and ride slowly home.

Garland couldn't fathom the mystery of Coryn's strange behaviour. From what she had seen, it seemed that he hadn't met another girl after all. But *something* had changed him. Something had made him turn cold towards her, and she didn't know what it could be.

Then, after ten days, she had a shock.

She had followed Coryn to the hill as usual. Today, though, he didn't pace around the stone circle but instead sat down on the grass and spent some two hours writing. He covered several sheets of paper – and when at last he rose to leave, one of the sheets fell from the bundle he carried and fluttered to the ground.

Garland's heartbeat quickened. Coryn had not noticed the dropped paper; he was striding away towards his horse and he did not look back. She waited, churning with impatience, until the soft thud of hoofs in the grass faded away, then she left her hiding place and ran up the hill.

The day had been bright but with patches of cloud, and as Garland reached the stone circle one cloud drifted across the sun. The light dimmed abruptly, sliding the world into dreary grey shade, and suddenly the Nine Men seemed to tower menacingly and almost accusingly above her, frowning down like a dark threat. Garland stopped, feeling gooseflesh break out on her arms. She had never been up here alone before, and she felt a sense of dread creep over her as she stared at the stones. In this peculiar light they looked almost human – almost *alive* – and she was afraid to step into the circle and be surrounded by their sinister shapes.

But the paper Coryn had dropped was lying in the circle, fluttering as the wind caught at it. She *must* retrieve it! Garland took a deep breath, then ran into the circle and snatched up the sheet, trying not to look again at the Nine Men. In the grass something rustled, making her jump. It was only a rabbit, or perhaps a vole, but for a moment it sounded like a stealthy footstep . . .

Garland darted out of the circle again and let out her breath in a thankful gasp. She hurried back to the safety of the trees, and only when she felt secure among the leaves did she at last look at the paper.

There, in Coryn's handwriting, was a

beautiful and moving love poem. Some of the words were unreadable, for in many places the page was stained with tears. But the inscription at the top was clear.

It read: *To my beloved Garland.*

Garland leaned back against a tree-trunk, her green eyes widening with astonishment and emotion. Coryn had written these words for her – he still loved her! In fact, so powerful was the tenderness and passion in the poem that it shook her to the core of her heart. There could be no doubt – Coryn had not met another girl; his love was as steadfast and intense as it had ever been.

Garland felt tears fill her eyes, just as they had filled Coryn's as he wrote. The knowledge that his love had not, after all, turned to hatred was an overwhelming comfort to her. But the sadness in his poem was so great that she ached with compassion. Though her greatest fear had been assuaged, she was certain now that something was terribly wrong in Coryn's life. Something so dreadful that he couldn't bring himself to confide in her.

She raised her wet face to the sky. The cloud had drifted away and the sun was shining again, but to Garland the brightness looked bleak and harsh. She must find out the truth. It was more vital now than ever – for if she could not help Coryn in his unhappiness, who could? He meant everything to her. She would find a way to tell him that, however great his trouble, she would stand at his side and be strong for him. Gently, kindly, she must persuade him to tell her everything. For until and unless she did, there would be no comfort for either of them.

Garland made her way home as solemnly as Coryn had done. Yet deep inside her was a little spark of hope. For in just a short time, on the night before the rising of the harvest moon, the annual Harvest Fair was to take place. There would be speeches, entertainments, music and dancing; everyone for miles around always attended, and Coryn would be no exception. At such an occasion he couldn't ignore Garland. They would dance together – it would be expected of them. And amid the festivities, there would surely be a chance for Garland to snatch a private moment with Coryn and persuade him to reveal the truth.

Her tears were drying on her cheeks and she felt better. The paper – Coryn's lovely poem – was hidden in her bodice, close to her heart. And Garland was resolved that nothing would stand in her way now. Whatever Coryn's trouble might be, together they would overcome it. That was all that mattered.

CHAPTER V

OST FESTIVALS in the district took place within sight of the stone circle, and the Harvest Fair was no exception. Held on a grassy meadow at the foot of the hill, the celebration began at sunset and continued all through the moonlight hours. People always flocked to the fair in great numbers, and the night-time setting gave it an atmosphere that was all its own.

The day had been hot, with a close, sultry feeling in the air. Pessimists said there would be a thunderstorm, but no clouds gathered, and as the sun sank and the first stars glittered in a clear sky the revels got under way.

The crowd streamed to the meadow, all dressed in their best clothes and eager for fun. There was much fun to be had, for a great many traders and entertainers had come to sell their wares or show off their talents, and a special dancing square had been roped off, with musicians ready on a makeshift platform. But for all the merriment there was something eerie about the scene. Music and laughter echoed strangely in the gathering dusk. Flickering torches and lanterns cast long, gaunt shadows that seemed to have a life of their own. And the brooding presence of the nine standing stones at the top of the hill was impossible to ignore. Despite the merriment, the stones cast a shadow on the occasion. As the fair began, the village elders carried an offering of new-baked bread and wine to the circle. In this way, they hoped, the spirits would not feel excluded from the festivities, and so would not cast a baneful influence over the night.

This year, too, there was something else to add to the sense of unease – for a group of Wanderers had come to the festivity. The Wanderers were pale-skinned and pale-haired people, who travelled the countryside and lived by secret laws of their own. They were renowned for their magical skills – they could foretell the future, cure sickness, cast spells. It was even whispered that, if they chose, they could make the sun shine at midnight. And though they were respected for their powers, they were also feared.

Garland saw the Wanderers' strangely decorated wagons, grouped half-way up the hill, when she arrived with her parents at the revel. For years the travelling people had not attended the Harvest Fair. Why, she wondered, had they chosen to come now? It was as if their presence was somehow significant, and each time she glimpsed one of them mingling with the crowd, she suppressed a little shiver of foreboding.

But it wasn't long before her attention was distracted from the Wanderers. The fair was in full swing. Sideshows drew crowds. Jugglers and acrobats cavorted, catching the coins that people threw to them. Hawkers bawled from every booth, proclaiming that *their* cakes or pies or trinkets were the best to be found anywhere. The dancing square was lit by torches on tall poles, and couples were already stepping out to the lively strains of jigs and reels. Garland's heart quickened as she thought of her plan, and she began to look about for Coryn.

Any hopes she had that Coryn's mood might have changed were soon dashed. From the moment he arrived with his mother at the festivities it was obvious that he had been reluctant to come at all. The widow greeted Garland warmly, though with an odd sadness that redoubled Garland's fears, but again Coryn seemed stiff and distracted. He had little to say, and every smile seemed to be an effort.

However, when Garland's father, who seemed to have noticed nothing amiss, said jovially that it was about time the two young people danced together, Coryn could find no excuse to refuse. Garland silently blessed her father as Coryn reluctantly took her hand and led her to join the dancers in the square.

The moon had risen high above the hill now, almost at the full, and its cool silver light brightened the festivities. The dancers were forming up for a reel, but Coryn's mind was clearly else-where, lost in a world of his own. Garland told herself to be patient and bide her time. When the dance ended, her chance would come.

Then, half-way through the dance, she saw the Wanderer woman . . .

She was standing at the edge of the square, pale and fey as a ghost; an ancient crone with white hair in long plaits that fell to her waist. She was dressed in a shabby gown that seemed to consist of extraordinary motley-coloured patches, with long scarves trailing over her shoulders and arms. And she was watching them.

Garland missed her step, but Coryn didn't seem to notice. The old woman was *staring*, and something about her sent a tremor down Gar-land's spine. Though her figure was stooped and withered, her eyes were intensely bright, seeming to fix Garland with a hypnotic look – and suddenly Garland was frightened.

Then someone bumped into them, and in the momentary confusion Garland turned her head away. When she looked back again, the Wand-erer woman had vanished.

The dance went on, but Garland's heart was no longer in it. The strange old woman had discon-certed her and she felt very uneasy. Nonetheless, when the music ended at last and they left the arena, she rallied herself and, as Coryn seemed about to walk away, grasped hold of his hand.

'Coryn, this can't go on any longer!' she said. 'I *have* to talk to you!'

He stopped, stood very still. 'What is it?'

Garland was determined not to be daunted this time, and she forced the words out in a rush.

'Coryn, please don't go on pretending any longer!' She squeezed his fingers. 'I know that there's some terrible trouble in your life, and that for some reason you don't want me to know about it. But I love you more than anything else in the world, and I want to help you! If you truly love me, as I believe you do, then you must trust me enough to confide in me! Whatever this secret is, it surely isn't so terrible that we can't face it together?'

For one moment, just one, she thought he would unbend and turn to her. But then he pulled his hand from her grip and pinched the bridge of his nose as though he was desperately weary.

'Garland, *stop* it,' he said quietly. 'I've told you before – there's nothing wrong.'

'But –'

'*No.*' He interrupted her vehemently. '*Please*, Garland. There's nothing to say. Nothing to do. I've told you before and I'll tell you again: everything's all right. Just believe that, and stop these pointless questions!'

And before Garland could say or do anything more, he swung away and strode into the crowd.

'*Coryn!*' Garland's anguished cry echoed through the night-lit fair and heads turned in surprise. But she ignored the stares; aware only of her misery and fury she plunged into the throng after Coryn, trying to catch up with him as he hurried away. Coryn had a long stride and was walking quickly; Garland broke into a run – and collided with someone who moved suddenly out of the crowd.

It was the old Wanderer woman. Shocked, but still remembering her manners, Garland started to say, 'I'm sorry –' but the crone interrupted her.

'You'll not save him by running, girl.' The woman's voice was husky and timeworn, and her strange, pale eyes seemed to pierce Garland's soul. 'Only by dancing.' Then she reached out a withered hand and touched her thumb to Garland's brow.

'I wish you the good luck you will need when the moon rises red,' the crone said. And before Garland could utter a sound, she turned and shuffled away.

Garland stared after her, stunned and a little frightened. Was the old woman mad? Or was there some awful significance in her cryptic words? She didn't understand!

She opened her mouth to call after the crone. But the cry caught in her throat as she glimpsed Coryn's mother standing a short way off. She was unaware of Garland's presence, but she had

36

seen the Wanderer woman. And her face bore a look of recognition – and of horror.

For several seconds Garland stared at the widow, who still hadn't noticed her. Suddenly the mystery had a new dimension – clearly Coryn's mother had encountered the crone before, and Garland wanted to run to her and beg her to explain. But before she could take a step towards her, the widow gave a great shudder and moved hurriedly away. And in Garland's few moments of uncertainty, both the crone and Coryn had also vanished.

Garland looked desperately around her. She had to find Coryn. She *had* to discover what the mystery was. She forged into the throng once more, to search for him.

But Coryn was nowhere to be found. At last, tired and bitterly unhappy, Garland gave up. All the hopes she had harboured tonight were dashed; there was no pleasure to be found in the fair and she wanted only to get away from the noise and lights and merriment and go home.

She and her parents left the hill at midnight, riding back under the glaring eye of the moon. Silently, Garland was railing against the old Wanderer woman. But for her, she would have caught up with Coryn; instead, her plans had ended in miserable failure. Yet, for all her anger, the crone's enigmatic words were coming back to haunt her. *You'll not save him by running. Only by dancing.* It made no sense! What could dancing have to do with this? And stranger still was that bizarre statement about the moon. *When the moon rises red* . . . It was utter nonsense. The moon was not red; it was white. It was *always* white.

Garland looked uneasily up at the sky, and the moon seemed to stare back at her, old and knowing and just a little sinister. But it *was* white. How could it possibly be anything else?

She shivered, and urged her pony on faster.

That night, Garland's dream came back. Once again she was two years old, and clutching at her mother in terror as *something* moved with ominous and terrible purpose along the night-black forest road outside. But this time, there was more . . .

Garland woke from the nightmare with a muffled cry of fright. For a while she lay still in the darkness, waiting for her racing pulse to slow and settle. And it was then, as her mind and body gradually calmed down, that she recalled that new and chilling detail which had appeared in her dream. For, in the moments before the menacing sounds began, she had been gazing out of the window. Gazing up at the moon.

And the moon was blood red.

Garland lay awake for the rest of the night, and by morning she had resolved what she must do. With the sun's early rays streaming in at her window she rose, dressed and went out into the garden where her mother was picking herbs.

'Mother,' Garland said, 'I had a strange dream last night.' She described the nightmare, then added, 'I wondered, Mother . . . was the dream real? When I was little, did it really happen?'

Her mother stood very still, and an odd frown appeared on her face. 'Why do you want to know, Garland?' she asked uneasily.

Garland told her about the strange encounter at the fair, and the old crone's words. To her surprise, her mother's expression grew angry.

'Those wretched Wanderer people!' she said. Her fist clenched, crushing the leaves she had picked. 'They're nothing but troublemakers who delight in frightening and misleading others!'

'But Mother, if what she said is true –'

'Of course it isn't true! You shouldn't listen to such foolishness, Garland. The old woman was talking nonsense. And your dream was just a dream, as I've told you before. It doesn't mean anything at all.'

Garland knew it would be useless to argue. But she also knew that her mother had not told her the whole truth. She *did* know more than she was prepared to say. And beneath her anger, Garland had seen another emotion.

Her mother was *frightened*.

All that day Garland worked about the house and garden. She tried to keep her worries and fears at bay, but as dusk fell they came creeping back into her mind, and at last she went up to her room and sat by the window. She had no answer to the mysteries that beset her, and no solution to the puzzle of Coryn.

Outside, the world was growing dark, and in the distance, beyond the hill where the Nine Men brooded, she could see the first glow of the rising moon. Tonight was the night of the harvest moon, and Garland watched as the glow grew brighter. She would wait, she thought, until the moon showed its face above the hill, and then she would go to bed and try to forget her troubles in sleep.

She settled on the window seat, resting her head against the wall. Minutes passed. Then, above the trees, above the hill and the circle of standing stones, slowly, steadily, the harvest moon rose.

And its face was not white, but an old, grim and gory red.

CHAPTER VI

GARLAND RAN ALONG the landing and all but hurled herself down the stairs and into the hall. Her heart was pounding agonizingly, and alarm churned through her mind like a tide. *The moon was red!* And she was certain now, beyond all doubt, that her mother knew some dreadful secret and was keeping it from her. Garland had to confront her. She had to know the truth!

Then, as she approached the door of the drawing-room, she heard her parents' voices on the other side.

They were arguing. Garland stopped in dismay, for she couldn't remember ever having heard them quarrel before. Her mother seemed to be pleading, and sounded tearful, while in her father's voice was a peculiar mixture of anger and worry.

Biting her lip, Garland crept up to the door and listened.

'It is *wrong* of us!' she heard her mother say. 'We should have told her, husband – we should have told Garland the truth from the beginning!'

'And risked losing all that we shall gain by the marriage?' her father retorted sharply.

'There'll be no marriage now! How can there be, when the sign is there in the sky for all to see?' Garland's mother stifled a sob. 'It had all worked out so well . . . we have money but no heritage; while Coryn and his mother are aristocratic but poor. It would have been the perfect match for both families! And now . . . now . . .' Her voice faltered. 'We *must* break the news to Garland. It's unfair to keep her in ignorance any longer!'

Her husband's voice rose again, fiercely. 'Don't be a fool, woman! What would we gain by telling her now? Neither she nor anyone else can stop what will happen. The only thing to do is make the best we can of it.'

'How?' Garland's mother asked tearfully.

'I'll go to see the widow, and talk to her. Even if the marriage can't take place, we might come to some other arrangement. Garland's dowry, perhaps, in exchange for a promise that she shall inherit the house and estate in Coryn's place. That way both we and the widow will have what we wanted.'

His wife made a choked sound. 'Is that the only thing you care about? What about poor Garland? This will break her heart!'

Garland's father snorted. 'You didn't worry about that when we made the betrothal agreement, so it's a little late to have pangs of conscience now! Garland's young; she'll get over her heartbreak soon enough. And with Coryn's house as a lure, there'll be no shortage of eligible young men willing to help her!'

There was a rustle of a silk skirt, and Garland, wide-eyed and holding her breath in shock and misery, could picture her mother standing up and pacing across the room.

'Very well,' she said at last, unsteadily. 'I suppose you're right, and we must make the best of it. But I wish . . .' Her voice tailed off.

'I know.' Her husband's tone softened a little. 'And don't think I'm not sorry for Garland – or for Coryn. But there's nothing we can do to change matters.'

'No,' Garland's mother agreed softly. 'We can't fight this power. They will take Coryn, just as they took his father all those years ago. And once again we must sit indoors, and keep the curtains drawn, and not look out as they go by.'

The two of them fell silent then, and outside the door Garland stood motionless, staring across the hall but seeing nothing. Horror was crawling through her – horror at what she had heard. She didn't understand it all, but what she *had* learned was more than enough to redouble the sick dread in her mind. Whatever Coryn's terrible secret was, her parents knew it. They had known all along, and they had deliberately kept it from her, in case it should spoil their own selfish plans! And the dream – her mother had lied to her, she knew that now, for those awful events of her nightmare really had happened.

And now, they were going to happen again . . . and this time they had some monstrous connection with Coryn.

Suddenly, footsteps sounded on the other side of the door, and quickly Garland drew back into the shadows. Moments later the door opened and her father appeared. From inside the room her mother said, 'It's late – can't you leave it until tomorrow?'

'There isn't time to wait,' Garland's father replied. 'She'll have seen the moon for herself. I must see her now, before it's too late.'

He strode across the hall to the front door. Garland watched as it shut behind him, and minutes later heard the clop of his horse's hoofs in the courtyard. He was going to see Coryn's mother . . . Garland crept out of hiding and stared at the drawing-room door. Her mother was still in there. And bleak anger rose in Garland as she thought of how her parents had deceived her; how they had used her and Coryn . . .

She moved to the door, opened it, walked in. Her mother's head came up sharply as she saw Garland, and quickly she tried to smile. But the smile was unconvincing and Garland said challengingly,

'Mother, don't pretend any more! I was outside the door just now. I heard what you and Father said.'

Her mother's face froze. Garland continued.

'You can't go on keeping the truth from me! If Coryn's in danger, I have a right to know! I want to *help* him!'

Her mother took refuge in an anger of her own. 'How dare you eavesdrop on us?' she demanded. 'It's wicked of you; it's –'

'*Wicked?*' Garland flared. 'No, Mother – what you and Father have done is wicked! You knew Coryn's secret from the beginning, didn't you? And you didn't tell me, because you feared it would spoil your plans.' Her hands started to shake. 'You wanted Coryn's family name, while his mother wanted your money. Nothing else mattered to you – not my happiness, not Coryn's, *nothing!*'

'It isn't like that, Garland,' her mother protested desperately. 'We wanted what was best for *you*.'

'Did you?' Garland cried. 'Then why didn't you tell me the truth, so that I could at least try to help Coryn?'

Her mother shook her head and looked away. 'It would have made no difference. You can't help him. No one can.'

'How do you know that? You might be wrong! Just tell me, Mother – tell me what's going to happen!'

She thought for a few moments that her mother would relent, for she stood very still, thinking. But then she looked back over her shoulder and said in a hard voice, 'No, Garland.

I won't tell you, for there's no point. What will be will be, and you must accept it. We must all accept it.'

'But I can't!' Garland cried. 'And if you and Father think I can, then you are both selfish and heartless and – and – *hateful!*'

'*Garland!*' There was real fury in her mother's voice. 'How *dare* you speak to me like that? Go to your room at once!'

For a single moment Garland stared back at her. Then she turned and fled out of the room and up the stairs.

Reaching her bedroom, Garland slammed the door and leaned against it, her heart pounding and thoughts racing. Her mother had refused to tell her the truth, and after this quarrel there was even less hope of persuading her. Very well then; there was only one thing to do. She would follow her father to Coryn's house. She would knock at the door, demand to be let in. Demand to *know*. However angry her father and Coryn's mother might be, they couldn't refuse her. They *couldn't*.

Garland ran to her ottoman and began to rummage through it for her outdoor clothes.

It was easy for Garland to slip out of the house unnoticed, but the journey that followed was a nerve-racking ordeal. She didn't dare to take her pony from the stables for fear that the noise might alert her mother, and so she was forced to make her way alone through the dark forest, following the path her father had taken. The light of the red moon was gloomy and deceptive, creating gaunt shadow-patterns of crimson and black that gave the trees a horrible semblance of life. All the familiar landmarks seemed changed by the eerie glow, and when Garland reached the open grassland the entire scene looked as if it was stained with blood. She couldn't find the courage to glance up at the moon – and she was even more afraid to look at the hill where the Nine Men stood bleak against the sky. Only the thought of Coryn's peril stopped her from turning and running back to the sanctuary of home.

At last, though, she reached Coryn's house. Her father's horse was tethered at the door, but there was no one to be seen, and only one window in the entire building was lit. It looked, Garland thought, like a house of ghosts, abandoned and grim. And suddenly she felt too afraid to approach any closer.

She stopped at the edge of the trees, trying to decide what to do. To have braved this night journey and then lose her nerve at the last moment was foolish – she *must* knock!

But then, suddenly, the front door opened and her father came out. Coryn's mother was with him; she looked as if she had been crying. Garland watched: her father was saying something, but the widow only shook her head in reply.

Then her father mounted his horse, and Garland dodged back into the deeper shadows as he started to ride away. If he saw her now, he would make her return home with him. She didn't want that. She would wait until he had gone, and then she would approach the house.

Her father passed by, and the sound of hoofs began to fade. Coryn's mother had gone inside, and Garland started to move from her hiding place –

Behind her, the undergrowth rustled.

Garland froze. Someone – or something – was creeping up on her . . . *what was it?* Her heart began to pound suffocatingly; she clenched her fists, took a deep breath – and swung round.

Among the trees, weird and spectral in the ruby light from the moon, a figure was standing. Garland's eyes widened as she recognized the white hair, motley clothes and wizened face of the old Wanderer woman she had encountered at the fair.

The crone gazed at Garland, steadily, knowingly. Then she raised one gnarled finger and beckoned. As if compelled by a power beyond her control, Garland moved slowly towards her until they were standing face to face. The crone smiled an enigmatic smile, and spoke in a voice that sounded like a bough creaking in the night breeze.

'You'll not help him in that way, dancing girl,' she said. 'Only nine ladies can save him from the

Nine Men. Nine ladies, and the old harvest dance.'

Then, with a swiftness that belied her age, the old woman turned and melted away into the forest.

For a moment Garland was too stunned to react. The Nine Men? What could the standing stones possibly have to do with the threat to Coryn? The old woman was talking in riddles –

Then suddenly her paralysis snapped. 'Wait!' she called. 'Wait, please – I don't understand what you mean!' She plunged in among the trees, pushing her way through low-hanging branches. 'Come back – oh, come back!'

But there was no answer. Like mist dissolving, the crone had vanished without trace.

Garland looked wildly around, shaking with shock and fear. Where could the old woman be? Then she remembered the Wanderers' wagons, gathered together on the hill of the stone circle. The thought of braving that place alone at night, and with the crone's mysterious warning about the Nine Men still ringing in her mind, was horrifying. But Garland knew she had no choice. She had to find the old woman again, and urge her to explain.

But when she reached the hill, the wagons were no longer there. Dismay eclipsed Garland's fear of the standing stones and she climbed the hill breathlessly to the place where they had been, praying that she would find some trace, some sign. Her prayers went unanswered. There were only wheel-tracks in the earth, and the imprint of horses' hoofs. The Wanderers had left as suddenly and secretively as they had arrived, and the tracks were so confused that she couldn't even tell which direction they had taken.

Garland began to shiver as a mixture of misery, tiredness and fear took hold of her. The gory moonlight steeped the night with a terrible sense of foreboding, and above her on the hilltop she could see the first and largest of the Nine Men, a huge, dark shape looming over her. In the gloom it looked almost human; like a tall and gaunt man standing with shoulders hunched. As if, suddenly, it might uproot itself and lurch menacingly down towards her . . .

Suddenly Garland's nerve snapped. With a cry of fright she turned and ran back down the hill, back towards the forest and home. She raced among the trees as though pursued by a hundred ghosts, and arrived at the house gasping with exhaustion. To her relief it seemed her absence hadn't been discovered, and she was able to get into the house by a back way and reach her room, where she fell on to the bed, sobbing stormily. What was she to do? She felt so *helpless!* Something terrible was going to happen to Coryn, and she didn't even know what it was, let alone how to prevent it! The only clues she had were the old Wanderer woman's cryptic message and the memory of her dream. It wasn't enough. It wasn't *enough!*

She turned over at last and stared at her window. The curtains were closed and so the moon was invisible. But she knew it was there, red as blood, a baleful power laughing down at her from the sky. And in that moment Garland hated it with all the power in her soul.

CHAPTER VII

GARLAND DIDN'T want to fall asleep, but emotion and weariness at last got the better of her, and she fell into a dismal slumber filled with confused nightmares. When she woke, sunlight was pouring in at her window, and with a shock she realized that it was nearly mid-morning. How could she have slept for so long? Hours had been lost; hours which might be vital. She had to see Coryn. She had to go back to his house at once – and this time, she would not leave until she knew the truth!

Her parents were having breakfast; she heard their voices as she came downstairs. After last night's confrontation with her mother it was vital that they knew nothing of her plans, so Garland tiptoed out by the back way, saddled her pony and within minutes was riding as fast as she could away from the house.

The forest looked very different this morning, green and friendly and filled with natural light. The crawling horrors of the night and the red moon were gone, but all the same Garland couldn't keep down a shiver as she galloped across the open grassland and saw the hill and the standing stones again. The crone's words rang in her memory: '*Only nine ladies can save him from the Nine Men* . . .'

Her mind spinning with unanswered questions, Garland reached Coryn's house. To her bewilderment a coach was drawn up at the front door, with two large cases loaded on its roof. The coachman was on his box seat; as Garland approached he flicked the reins and the coach began to move, and Garland glimpsed a white face inside. Coryn's mother – was Coryn with her? Horrified, Garland spurred her pony forward. She slewed into the coach's path and leapt from the saddle as the coachman pulled up with a startled shout.

'Coryn!' Garland rushed to the coach window. 'Coryn, where are you going –?' Then she stopped. For Coryn's mother was alone inside.

They stared at each other, Garland's eyes pleading, the widow's haunted. Then, softly, Coryn's mother said, 'You shouldn't have come, Garland. It would be kinder to Coryn if you went away, as I am doing.'

'You're *leaving?*' Garland's voice shook.

'Yes. For a little while. Until it is over.' The widow put a clenched fist to her mouth, forcing back tears. 'I don't want to. But Coryn begged it of me. And I can't refuse the last promise I will ever make to my son.'

Garland's pulse raced suffocatingly. 'Please,'

she said fervently, 'please, you *have* to explain! Tell me what's going to happen to Coryn!'

But the widow shook her head. 'The less you know, the better it will be,' she replied. She started to close the window, then paused. 'However much it hurts us, Garland, we must both try to forget Coryn now. For tonight the Nine Men will come to life. They will kill my son, just as they killed his father all those years ago. And there is nothing we, or any living soul, can do to stop them.'

As Garland's eyes widened in horrified disbelief, the widow called to the coachman, 'Drive on!' The whip cracked; the horses began to move, and Garland was forced to jump back. Coryn's mother turned her head and looked at Garland one last time.

'You and he would have been so happy . . .' she said, her voice breaking. And Garland was left standing alone before the house as the coach turned on to the forest road.

'I know you're there!' Garland cried. 'Oh, Coryn, open the door! *Please!*'

Her fists pounded again on the solid wood. She must have been hammering for ten minutes, ever since the coach had disappeared from view. But Coryn had refused to answer.

At last, though, she heard sounds from within the house. Slow, reluctant footsteps. She held her breath, praying silently. Then the bolt drew back, the door opened, and Coryn stood before her.

He looked immaculate, dressed in fresh clean clothes and with his hair neatly combed. But his face was deathly white, and the blue of his eyes had faded to a chill, bleak shade without the smallest trace of hope.

He said: 'Garland . . .' And his voice was no longer hostile but filled with emotion.

'Oh, Coryn!' She stumbled over the threshold before he could change his mind and close the door again, and tried to put her arms round him. But he pushed her gently back. 'Don't, Garland, please,' he said. 'It only makes things worse.'

'How can they be any worse than this?' Garland cried. 'You mother told me that you're going to die! She said –'

He interrupted almost angrily. 'She shouldn't have said anything! I didn't want you to know, Garland. Don't you understand?' Suddenly he covered his face with his hands. 'I tried to make you stop loving me. That's why I was so cold towards you. I thought – I hoped – that it would make the pain less for you.'

Tears filled Garland's eyes. 'Oh, Coryn,' she said. 'I could never stop loving you! You should have trusted me – you should have *told* me!' Desperately, she clutched at his arm. 'Perhaps it isn't too late even now! Together, we might –'

'No.' He said it sharply. 'It *is* too late. This is my destiny; I can't change it, and neither can you. If you knew the whole story, you'd realize that and accept it.'

Garland gripped him ferociously, almost shaking him as her emotions boiled over. 'How can I accept when I don't *know* the story?' she protested wildly. 'No one will explain! Please, Coryn, *please* – don't hide the truth from me any longer! If you're going to die –' she almost choked on the word, 'then don't I have the right to at least know *why?*'

For a moment she thought that Coryn would pull away and turn his back on her. But abruptly his shoulders slumped, and all the anger seemed to drain out of him.

'Oh, my love . . .' he whispered. 'Yes. It's true; you have the right to know. Though I wanted so much to spare you . . .'

'I don't want to be spared,' said Garland, crying now.

Coryn nodded. 'Come into the drawing-room,' he said. 'My mother has sent the servants away; no one will disturb us. I'll tell you the tale, Garland. I'll tell you all of it.' He pressed a hand to his eyes. 'It will be such a relief . . .'

Their betrothal ceremony had taken place in the drawing-room. And it was there that this whole unhappy chain of events had begun . . . Garland suppressed a shiver, pushing away the memory, and let him lead her across the hall.

*

'It began centuries ago,' Coryn said. 'All this land was wild wood then. But one of my ancestors decided to make his home here. He cleared part of the wood for his estate, and he started to build this house. Then, while he was building it, he found a grove of trees near by – on the hill where the Nine Men stand.'

Garland's eyes widened. Coryn continued.

'The trees grew in the middle of the stone circle, and they were so beautiful that my ancestor wanted to use them in his house. So he cut them down. And that was his terrible mistake.'

An awful sense of premonition was beginning to creep through Garland. Softly, she asked, 'What happened?'

Coryn smiled bitterly. 'The Nine Men *are* more than just standing stones,' he said. 'Each one contains a spirit. And the nine spirits had nine consorts. Those consorts lived within the trees that my ancestor cut down.'

Garland gasped, feeling a chill prickle break out on her skin. The old Wanderer woman had spoken of 'Nine Ladies' – could these be the spirits of the trees, the consorts of the Nine Men?

Coryn told her, then, the rest of the grim tale. Unbeknown to his ancestor, each year the Nine Men had come to life on the night of the harvest moon, to dance with their ladies in the stone circle. But when the trees were cut down, their ladies were lost to them. And in their rage the Nine Men were determined to punish the family who had stolen their beloveds away. From this day on, they decreed, the family must watch each year for the harvest moon. If it should be red, then on the following night the spirits of the stones would come to life again and claim a fee from the household. If the fee was paid, all would be well. But if it was not, then the Nine Men would come down from the hill to claim the life of the head of the household.

For a long time, Coryn told Garland, it seemed the fee was paid, as for many generations the house was happy, and great dances were held there and at the stone circle. But then things changed. One of Coryn's ancestors was killed, together with his wife, in a riding accident. Their son was only five years old; too young to have been told about his family's obligation. He grew up, married and had a family of his own – and then a year came when the harvest moon rose red. The young man knew nothing of what the Nine Men would demand from him, and so the fee was not paid. The spirits of the stones came for him, and killed him. And since then, with the knowledge of the fee lost, every eldest male of the family had died young, slain by the vengeful stones.

Trembling, Garland whispered, 'Didn't anyone else know what the fee should have been?'

Coryn shook his head. 'No. The secret was kept closely in the family; that, I think, was part of the bargain my first ancestor made.' He suppressed a shudder. 'And now I must pay the penalty, like my father and grandfather and many more before them. I must die, Garland.' He swallowed. 'Tonight, the Nine Men will come to life. They will march to this house to claim me, and no power in the world can save me from them.'

With a certainty that chilled her to the bone, Garland understood her dream at last. The awful sound she had heard, like the tramping of grim, unhuman feet – it had been the sound of the Nine Men passing by on the forest road. Thirteen years ago, they had made that journey, to challenge and kill Coryn's father. And tonight . . .

'*No!*' She choked the word out, desperately trying to deny the appalling truth. 'No, Coryn!' Tears started to stream down her face and she clung to him. 'I can't give up hope, for I love you too much to lose you! There *must* be a way to turn the curse aside and stop this!'

Gently Coryn took her face between his hands and gazed into her eyes. 'If only there were,' he said. 'But it's hopeless. Even our love can't conquer the power of the stones. I must die. It's inevitable. And you must go away, and try to forget me.'

'I can never do that!' she cried. 'I shall –'

'No.' He touched one finger to her lips, silencing her. 'Listen to me, my love. I've sent my mother and the servants away, for their own sakes. And now, if you truly love me, you must go, too. I mean to saddle my horse and ride in the forest one last time. I want to be alone, to make my final peace with myself and with the world.' His hands slipped down to her shoulders and his lips touched hers tenderly, lovingly, and with a longing that made Garland ache with grief. When at last they drew apart once more, Coryn added with an emotion that nearly shattered Garland's heart, 'My darling Garland, this is – it *must* be – our last goodbye.'

CHAPTER VIII

GARLAND STUMBLED through the forest, her pony following at her heels. Coryn's tears and her own were mingled and drying on her cheeks, and the memory of his last kiss burned in her mind like fire. She was numb with shock, horror and grief, and neither knew nor cared where her feet were taking her. Nothing mattered, *nothing*, save for the hideous knowledge that, tonight, she would lose her beloved Coryn for ever.

It would have been better, she told herself with bitter anguish, if he *had* fallen in love with another girl, as she had at first suspected. She would never, ever have got over that – but at least Coryn would still be alive. Now, though, there was not even that comfort. He was going to die. Only by discovering the secret of the Nine Men's ancient fee could she hope to save him. And the secret was forgotten, lost in the distant past and beyond her reach. There was nothing in all the world that she could do.

The forest before her was blurred by the tears that streamed from her eyes. Abruptly Garland realized that she had reached a clearing. In the clearing, brightly coloured against the green of the trees, stood a group of wagons. And by the wagons were people, with white skins and strange, pale hair . . .

Garland stopped, her pulse quickening. The Wanderers! So they hadn't left the district after all! A sudden wild hope surged violently in her, and she looked desperately around for the crone. But there was no sign of the old woman, and the Wanderers only stared back at her, their expressions giving no clue to their thoughts.

'P-please . . .' Garland stammered. 'Oh, please, can't you help me?'

No one answered; they only continued to gaze. Then, as though by some eerie telepathy, they all turned their heads away.

But as they did so, one young girl paused for a moment. Her mouth curved in a strange, sad smile – and she pointed, silently, into the depths of the forest.

Garland's heart seemed to turn over under her ribs. Was this a message, a clue? She didn't know, but in her desperation she had to take the chance. Tugging on her pony's reins, she turned and plunged back among the trees, following the direction that the girl had indicated.

This part of the forest was unfamiliar, the paths little used and very overgrown. Garland saw no trace of anyone, and soon she began to feel frightened. It seemed she had mistaken the girl's meaning, and that the gesture was merely a sign that the Wanderers wanted her to go away and leave them alone. There was nothing here that could help her. And if she went much further, she would be lost.

Then, among the birdsong and the rustling of leaves, she heard a new sound. Ahead of her, invisible in the greenery, someone was singing.

In a quavering voice, Garland called out, 'Hello . . .? Who's there?'

There was no answer, but the singing continued. The pony whickered uneasily; Garland stroked its nose to calm it, then moved cautiously forward.

Sunlight dappled down through the trees, casting pools of gold and shadow into another, smaller, clearing. And there, alone, was the old Wanderer woman.

Garland gasped and was about to rush forward . . . but then she halted as she realized that the crone was unaware of her presence. She was in a trance; her eyes were open, but she saw nothing. And as she sang, she was dancing. Her dance was stately and graceful, and she held out both arms in a curving gesture, as though embracing a partner. Garland's heart lurched with pain as she remembered how often she had danced with Coryn in just such a way. She thought she would start to cry again – until, suddenly, her ears caught the words of the old woman's song. And as their significance sank in, she froze.

To a curious, haunting little tune, the crone sang:

> *Dance the dance and step the measure,*
> *Nine for joy and nine for pleasure.*
> *Our delight shall be your treasure –*
> *Let the dance go on for ever.'*

With a shock that sent a shuddering wave through her, Garland's mind flew back to Coryn's house, and the carved frieze above the door to the neglected ballroom. *Dance the dance and step the measure* – it was Coryn's family motto!

Suddenly the old woman stopped dancing. For a few moments she stood absolutely still . . . then, in an instant, her trance snapped and her eyes focused on Garland's face. Garland opened her mouth to speak, but quickly the old woman raised a finger to her own lips, warning her to be silent. Like something from a strange dream, her voice reached Garland's ears.

'I can show you no more, dancing girl,' she said. 'But if you are wise, you may still save him.'

Stunned, Garland blinked. And when she looked again, the clearing was empty.

For a minute or more Garland stood motionless, her mind and body paralysed. But somewhere deep within her, a new feeling was stirring. A feeling so powerful that she hardly dared believe in it. A feeling of *hope* . . .

Coryn's family motto. It was the vital clue. It *had* to be! In the strange, cryptic and magical way of the Wanderers, the old woman had set her on the path that could solve the mystery and save her beloved's life. She must go back to Coryn, Garland told herself, and together they must strive to unravel the secret of the Nine Men's fee!

With a cry, she broke free of the thrall that held her, and gathered up her pony's reins, scrambling into the saddle. The pony pranced, catching her excitement, and Garland swung it round to face the way she had come. Her heels dug into its flanks, and she set off, as fast as the forest track would allow, towards Coryn's house.

Again Garland's knocking wasn't answered, but this time she knew Coryn was not hiding from her. He had gone – he had saddled his horse and left for his last ride through the forest. Garland knew that she would have little chance of finding him, and she was frantic. He might be gone for hours, and the position of the sun told her that it was already well past noon. What to do? She couldn't give up now!

There was only one chance, Garland thought. If Coryn was not here to help her, then she must search the house alone, and look for any clue, however small. Hastily tethering her pony she began to explore the outside of the building, hoping against all hope to find an open window. But the house was tightly closed up, doors and windows all barred and bolted. At last, breathless, fingernails broken from scrabbling at latches, legs scratched even through her long skirt by the brambles in the tangled garden, Garland stopped her useless search. She would have to do something more drastic.

She found a good-sized stone, took a deep breath, and hurled it at the nearest window. The crash of shattering glass set birds squawking in the trees, and Garland slid one arm carefully through the broken pane, fumbling for the window catch. The casement swung open, and, quick as a cat, she scrambled on to the sill and dropped down on the other side.

She found herself in the dining-room. The table was bare, and everything looked bleak and empty. Where to begin? The house was so big, and for a moment Garland's resolve almost failed her as she realized the size of her task. But she pushed the feeling down. For Coryn's sake, she mustn't lose heart now!

She began to search.

Hours later, Garland was on the verge of admitting defeat. She had scoured the house from top to bottom, combing rooms, rummaging in cupboards and drawers, even looking under rugs and behind pictures in her frenzied quest for anything, *anything* that might lead her in the right direction. And she had found nothing at all.

She finally ended up in the great hall, where doors led to the various downstairs rooms. The sun was slanting in at the big west window, and with a shock she realized how late the day was growing. She had only a few short hours now until moonrise, and she had made no progress whatever.

She looked towards the locked door of the disused ballroom. This was the one place she hadn't searched, for she had no key and the only way in would be to break one of the great windows from outside. She had been afraid to do that, and so had left the ballroom till last, hoping and praying that she would find what she needed elsewhere. Now though, she had no other choice. She had to get in.

She started towards the front door . . . then paused as a peculiar instinct prickled in her mind. The words the old Wanderer woman had sung were carved into the frieze above the ballroom door. Could the desperately needed clue lie there, rather than in the ballroom itself . . .?

She moved closer and stared at the frieze. *Dance the dance, and step the measure.* But there was something else carved into the wood. Something she had never noticed before. A small mark, like an arrow . . .

Garland ran to fetch a chair, placed it under

the doorway and scrambled up to look at the frieze more closely. The mark *was* an arrow, pointing down towards the floor. The floor? The flagstones? Dismay filled Garland, for even if there should be something hidden beneath the stones, they were far too heavy for her to prise up.

But then it occurred to her that her guess was wrong. It might – it just might – be that the arrow meant she should look not to the floor, but at the other side of the frieze . . .

Her heart began to thump, and she reached up to the frieze, trying to wrest it from the wall. One nail gave way, and Garland swayed precariously, almost losing her balance as the cumbersome wooden carving started to slip down. She steadied herself, drew a deep, determined breath, and with a powerful effort pulled the frieze free. It was a dead weight on her arms, but she was able to lower it down without harm, and eagerly she turned it over.

Words were carved on the other side. Far more words. And as Garland peered, she recognized them. This was the song the Wanderer woman had been singing. But not merely the one line of the motto, nor even the one verse she had heard. Here, the song was complete. And as she began to read, Garland realized with mounting excitement that, at last, she had found the vital clue!

The song ran:

Dance the dance and step the measure,
Nine for joy and nine for pleasure.
Our delight shall be your treasure –
Let the dance go on for ever.

When the crimson moon rides free,
Call our ladies, three times three,
Take a piece from every tree;
Dance the dance, and pay the fee.

Oak and elm and aspen grey,
Briar, willow, blackthorn, may,
Birch and beech; let none delay!
And dance with us till break of day.

Keep the promise, keep it true,
And this shall be our pledge to you:
Your blessings many, sorrows few,
In all you are and all you do.

But if the promise you should break,
Another pledge the Nine shall make,
And we shall come, and we shall take
Your life in payment, for their sake.

Garland stared and stared at the frieze as the significance of what she had found came slowly home to her. This was far more than a mere clue – this was the *answer*! The key to summoning back the Nine Ladies, and thus fulfilling the pledge that Coryn's distant ancestor had made to the spirits of the stone circle! In clear words, the song spelled out what must be done if the

Nine Men were to be placated: 'Take a piece from every tree; dance the dance, and pay the fee.'

But then Garland's excitement was eclipsed by a slow, cold wave of horror. 'Every tree' meant, clearly, the nine trees that once had grown in the grove, and where the Nine Men's consorts had lived. But how could she take a piece from every one of those trees? For the trees were long gone.

Or were they? Of course, Garland thought; of course! Coryn's ancestor had cut down the Nine Ladies' trees – but he had used them in the building of this house. Those ancient trunks were not lost for ever. They were still here. But where? Among the roof-timbers? In the foundations? In the beams of a wall or ceiling? *Where?*

Then, like a glorious sunrise in her mind, Garland understood. There was only one place where the Nine Ladies' trees could be. The ballroom – the beautiful, abandoned ballroom which she had never seen. The answer must lie there!

Again she started to run towards the door, thinking to break into the ballroom from outside. But she had taken no more than two paces when she heard a sound behind her. A faint but emphatic *click*.

Garland spun round. There was no one there, and nothing had apparently moved in the hall. But then, as her gaze lit on the ballroom door, she saw the handle quiver slightly. With no visible hand to touch it, the handle turned . . . and the ballroom door began slowly to swing back on its hinges.

Terror and excitement boiled into Garland's mind. Some strange power was at work here; the power, perhaps, of the house itself . . . or of what lay within it. It had released the lock – that was the click she had heard. And now it was calling her to enter the ballroom . . .

Slowly, hardly daring to breathe, Garland moved towards the door, and reached out to push it fully open.

CHAPTER IX

GARLAND STOPPED on the threshold of the ballroom and stared in awe at the scene before her. The room was huge; far larger even than the great chamber where her fateful betrothal party had been held. And she could see that it had once been beautiful, with its tall, arched windows, elegant silver candle sconces and fine tapestries. But the beauty was shrouded now in grime and greyness. The windows were curtained not with velvet but with great swathes of cobwebs that dimmed the light to a grim, perpetual dusk. Dust lay thick on the floor, drifting in little eddies around Garland's feet. The candles were gone, the sconces tarnished from silver to black. In the far corner an old spinet stood forlorn and forgotten, its fine, once-polished lines now dulled and dark.

And set in a circle around the edge of the room were the carved pillars that Coryn had once described to her. In the gloom they looked like trees, as though the forest itself were encroaching on the house and creeping in. And, as intuition set her heart pounding anew, Garland began to count them.

There were nine pillars. Nine pillars, made from nine different woods.

Oak and elm and aspen grey; briar, willow, blackthorn, may . . . Garland stepped into the ballroom and drew closer to the carved columns. Softly, and with great care, she moved round the ballroom until she had examined every one.

'Oh, yes . . .' she whispered. 'Oh, *yes* . . .' Born and bred in the forest as she was, she knew all the many woods of the wildland. And the nine trees of the rhyme were all here.

She returned to the first pillar and looked at it more closely. There, all but invisible, were old, tiny scars, where slivers of the wood had been cut away long, long ago. Her heart soared. There could be no doubt now – she had found the Nine Ladies' trees!

But though she had succeeded in her quest, the danger was not yet over. And she was racing against time. The ballroom was darkening still further as the daylight outside deepened from gold to rose. Before long the sun would set – and soon after that it would be moonrise. Garland ran from the ballroom, ran to the kitchen where she snatched up the sharpest knife she could find. Returning, she hurried back to the pillars and began to cut a new sliver from each one. But as she worked, her hand started suddenly to tremble as she realized that, even when she held the precious prizes in her hands, she didn't know what she must do with them. *Take a piece from every tree*, the rhyme said. Yes, yes, she had done that! Then: *Dance the dance, and pay the fee*. But how was she to pay? What was the dance, and who must dance it? The song did not tell her.

The last sliver was cut, and Garland's fist closed convulsively around the tiny pieces of wood. She stared at the ballroom, at the dust and the cobwebs and the fading light which was turning to an eerie, deathly shade.

'What now?' Her own voice echoed in the stillness as, beseechingly, she asked the question aloud. 'Oh, please, wherever you are – whatever you are – tell me what I must do!'

But there was no one and nothing to answer her. Only the silence of the gathering evening.

Garland began to shiver, and her mind whirled frenziedly. She must *think!* She had the key: she had the payment that must be made. But it wasn't enough! And unless she could solve the last mystery, then the moon would rise, and the Nine Men would stir into awful life and start their long, malevolent march down from the hill . . .

Garland froze as a wild thought came to her. The Nine Men on the hill – was *that* the answer to her question? Must she take the slivers of wood to the circle, and make an offering of them to the standing stones?

Her blood chilled as she pictured herself climbing that foreboding hill in the gathering dusk and facing the gaunt shapes of the Nine Men, knowing as she did what was about to happen. But angrily she took a grip on herself. If her courage failed now, then what Coryn must face on this fateful night would be a thousand times more horrific than anything she might endure. What sort of coward was she, to even *think* of herself while he was still in peril of his life?

Garland put the slivers of wood carefully into the pocket of her riding coat, and looked at the ballroom one last time. She would have given all she possessed to find another solution, another way. But she could think of nothing else that might work.

Her fists clenched and she shut her eyes briefly. '*Oh please,*' she whispered, not knowing what powers might be listening but hoping that, somewhere, *some* benevolent force would hear her. '*Protect me, and help me to find the courage I need. And please, please, let my plan work!*'

Her eyes opened again. The ballroom was as empty and silent as ever. Garland suppressed a shiver, then turned and ran towards the front door.

The sun was sinking as Garland urged her pony along the forest track. When she reached the stretch of open grass, the sky and land alike were tinged blood-red by the last rays. At the edge of the trees Garland jumped from the saddle, tethered the pony and stood for a few moments staring at the hill. It looked dark and threatening against the sky. And the silhouettes of the Nine Men seemed to glower back at her like living enemies.

Steeling herself, Garland started up the hill. As she approached the stones a leaden, oppressive feeling filled her, and fear began to crawl through her every nerve. Dusk was falling rapidly, and in the east the first stars were already glittering. Soon the moon would show its face above the horizon. And then the true ordeal would begin.

She reached the hilltop and stopped at the edge of the stone circle. What should she do now? What was expected of her – what would *work?* Garland didn't know, but instinct prompted her to wait. When the moon rose: that would be the time.

She didn't dare step in among the stones, but instead crouched on the grass just outside the circle. Her heart was beating fast and she couldn't stop trembling. But she had to stay.

Minutes passed. The sun vanished, the afterglow began to fade, and darkness crept eerily over the land. The night was sultry and still, but Garland shivered as though bitterly cold. It was so *quiet* here. The birds had stopped singing; there wasn't even a murmur of wind to break the silence.

Then she saw that on the eastern skyline a

glow had appeared. The moon was rising. Slowly, slowly, it showed its face above the horizon. Not a red moon tonight, but white and chill and sinister, a cold, cruel eye staring down at the world. The moonlight fell on the standing stones, and long shadows stretched out towards Garland, like spectral fingers reaching to clutch at her.

Shaking, her pulse racing, Garland rose to her feet. She took a step forward, another, another . . . and entered the stone circle.

And as she reached the circle's centre, the moon-shadows around her shifted.

Garland looked quickly at the nearest stone, and her thudding heart lurched and almost stopped altogether. For the stone was *changing*. Gradually, horrifyingly, its rough outlines were becoming sharper, taking on detail. At the top, a face was forming; proud, hawk-nosed, quartz eyes glittering fiercely under heavy brows. And below the face were carved shoulders, a body, strong legs – the stone was flowing and twisting, forming the figure of a man. As Garland turned her head in dawning horror, she saw that the other stones, too, were transforming. Carved hair gleamed like basalt in the unearthly moonlight. Harsh faces glared at the night.

And with a weird, grating sound, nine heads turned to stare down the hill towards Coryn's house.

Garland stood transfixed in the middle of the

circle. She felt sick with sheer terror, and couldn't move a muscle. The legend was coming true – the Nine Men were waking from their long sleep!

There was another awful sound, a rasping and rumbling like rocks clashing together. The tallest of the figures rocked, lurched, and one stone foot tore free of the ground. One by one the others dragged their feet clear. Then, as though at some unspoken signal, they all began to lumber inexorably towards the slope of the hill.

Suddenly Garland's horror turned to panic. They were going. The Nine Men were starting their march to Coryn's house. And she had stood transfixed, doing nothing –

'No!' Her voice rang out shrilly. 'No, wait! Stop, please stop!' She held her hands out, displaying the slivers of wood she had cut from the pillars. 'I . . . I have brought them! The pieces from your ladies' trees! I have the fee!'

Garland didn't know what would happen as she cried out. The Nine Men might turn on her; they might mow her down and trample her body into the grass. But in this frantic moment her own safety meant nothing. All that mattered was saving Coryn, and as one of the stone figures tramped towards her she stumbled into its path, trying to show and offer the slivers.

The figure ignored her. It moved heavily past as though she were not even there. The others followed. They paid her not the slightest heed. They didn't even turn their heads to look at her as they began to march down the hill.

Dazed, Garland could only stare as the last nightmarish shape passed by. The Nine Men couldn't see her. To them, she didn't even exist, for their terrible, unhuman minds were fixed on one thing – their age-old vengeance against Coryn's family.

Hardly aware of what she was doing, she started to follow the living statues. She had tried the only plan she could think of, and it had failed. What else could she *do*? What would make the Nine Men see her and listen to her?

The stone figures were almost at the bottom of the hill now, and Garland stumbled after them. She felt as if she were caught up in a nightmare from which she couldn't wake. Surely, her mind pleaded silently, *surely* there must be another way to help Coryn? But she could think of nothing. And time was running out.

The Nine Men reached the foot of the hill. Garland's pony whinnied with fright, but they took no more notice of it than they had of Garland as they lumbered towards the forest track. Garland followed helplessly, as though in a trance. She remembered her dream again; the darkness, the terror, the relentless footsteps in the night. Now, the dream was coming hideously true once more. For soon the Nine Men would pass her own home, just as they had done on that fateful night thirteen years ago.

Suddenly Garland stopped, and a shudder went through her as she realized that she had been hypnotized by the stones' awful spell. She must go to Coryn! However hopeless her bid might be, she must try, still try, to save him somehow! And if she failed, then she must find the courage to stand beside him when the Nine Men came, and be with him to the last!

The monstrous shapes were moving among the trees, and the rhythmic sound of their footfalls became muffled and ominous as the leaves shrouded them. They were taking the main track through the forest, but Garland knew of a short cut. On horseback, she could reach Coryn's house before they did, and abruptly she swung round and raced towards her pony. The pony was prancing, pulling at its tether and still afraid, but she untied it and scrambled into the saddle. Where was the other path? She looked wildly around, then saw it, a narrow, twisting trail half-hidden by undergrowth. It would be hard to follow in the darkness. But it was her only hope now.

Garland swung the pony's head round; then her heels dug fiercely into its flanks, and they plunged into the moon-dappled dark of the woodland.

CHAPTER X

GARLAND'S RIDE through the forest was a nerve-racking test of her daring. In bright daylight the path was difficult enough; by night there were hazards at every turn. Briars and brambles tangled the track. Low branches hung down from the trees or reached out to snatch at her. And worst of all was the peril of fallen trunks that lay in her way and couldn't be seen in the darkness until she was almost on top of them. But in her desperation Garland had no thought for the risks. She spurred the pony to greater and greater effort, swerving here, ducking there, clinging on as they jumped yet another obstacle. Every twist of the track brought the fear of a crashing fall – but suddenly she glimpsed brighter moonlight ahead, and moments later they burst out of the forest and Coryn's house was before them.

Garland pulled the pony to a sliding, whinnying halt and all but fell out of the saddle. Dropping the reins, she began to run towards the house – then stopped.

The moon shone coldly down, and by its glare she saw that a pale, solitary figure was standing before the house. Garland's heart gave a pulsing thump as she recognized Coryn. And Coryn in his turn stared at her with shock and dismay.

'Garland!' He took a step backwards. 'Why have you come here? You mustn't stay! You have to go away!'

'I won't go!' Garland cried. 'I won't leave you to face this alone!' She started towards him, reaching out, but he gripped her wrists and held her at arm's length.

'No, Garland!' His face and voice were tormented. 'If you love me, do what I ask! Leave me to my fate!'

She shook her head violently. 'I can't give up hope!'

'But there *is* no hope,' Coryn said. 'Don't you understand?' His eyes gazed into hers, and they were bleak. 'The Nine Men are on their way here, and nothing can stop them. Leave me, Garland. Go into the house and leave me here alone. *Please.*'

With these last words Coryn released her and turned away. Garland reached out towards him again, meaning to argue further, but as she began to move, something stirred in the depths of her mind. Like a warning – or an alert. And she seemed to hear the voice of the old Wanderer echoing in her memory.

'*You'll only save him by dancing . . .*'

Dancing . . . She swung round. The old ballroom lay directly in front of her. Moonlight was shining on its great windows, and the panes seemed to glow like strange jewels. And a wild idea came suddenly, shockingly to Garland.

She flung a swift, agonized glance in Coryn's direction. 'Coryn, I –' she began to say, then abruptly realized that there was no time to try to explain to him, even if she could have found the words. Besides, he wouldn't believe her. She didn't know if she dared believe herself. But she had to *try*.

Garland ran to the house, plunged through the open front door and rushed to the ballroom. The windows, lit even through their grime by the moon, shone like spectral mirrors, and patterns of silver and black scattered across the floor. Shadows flowed over Garland as she reached the centre of the room, and there she halted, drawing a deep breath. The tune – what was the tune? Desperately she tried to recall the old woman's voice again, but it wouldn't come. Perhaps, she thought, if she began to recite the words of the song, then she would remember the melody –

In a quavering voice that echoed hollowly in the empty ballroom, she began to speak:

> *'Dance the dance and step the measure,*
> *Nine for joy and nine for pleasure.*
> *Our delight shall be your treasure –*
> *Let the dance go on for ever . . .'*

Yes – oh, yes, it was coming back! Garland's heart started to pound with a hope that she hardly dared acknowledge, and her voice rose again, singing this time as the tune the Wanderer woman had sung flooded into her mind.

> *'When the crimson moon rides free,*
> *Call our ladies, three times three,*
> *Take a piece from every tree;*
> *Dance the dance, and pay the fee.'*

Her feet were moving now, almost without her willing them to. First one step, then another, slow at first but gradually quickening. The steps of a dance . . .

'Oak and elm and aspen grey,' sang Garland, her voice stronger now, 'Briar, willow, blackthorn, may; birch and beech, let none delay! And dance with us till break of day!'

And then, out of the air, she seemed to hear strains of unearthly music, blending with her singing in a sweet, eldritch harmony. It was faint, and so fragile that the slightest breath might dissolve it, but at the sound of it Garland's spirit leaped with joy. Her flash of intuition had been true – the song *was* a spell! And the spell was beginning to work!

Suddenly Garland's feet seemed to tug her towards the old spinet at the far side of the room. She ran to it and tried to lift the lid. At first it wouldn't come; it was caked with dust and grime and had stuck. But she persevered, and suddenly with a creak it freed itself. Swiftly Garland brushed aside the spiders' webs that festooned it like some strange and sad decoration, then she put her fingers on the keyboard and played a chord. The spinet was badly out of tune, but instinct told her that didn't matter. She must play! She must answer the ethereal music with music of her own!

Tentatively at first, but soon with growing confidence, Garland began to play the ancient melody, and her voice soared up as she sang with all the power of her churning emotions.

> *'Keep the promise, keep it true,*
> *And this shall be our pledge to you:*
> *Your blessings many, sorrows few,*
> *In all you are and all you do.'*

As she reached the end of the verse, the spectral harmonies swelled to a crescendo, and suddenly, stunningly, the ballroom was filled with music. Garland gasped aloud as a surge of power seemed to pulse through the room. It took hold of her, snatched her hands from the spinet and, with a giddying magic that she couldn't resist, spun her away back to the middle of the floor. The music played faster, more urgently, and like a leaf in a gale Garland began to dance. Round the ballroom she whirled, faster, faster, hair and skirt flying, arms outspread and a cloud of dust kicking up in her wake. She couldn't control herself; she was impelled by the dizzying power of the music. The room seemed to spin around her, light and shadows flicking past in a mad zig-zag, and in the eerie light she could almost believe that the nine pillars were moving too, swaying in rhythm with the melody. Her feet were like quicksilver, her body felt weightless, she was dizzy, breathless –

Then, so abruptly and unexpectedly that she cried aloud in shock, the music stopped. Silence crashed down on the ballroom, and Garland stumbled to a gasping, bewildered halt.

What had happened? Alarm filled her and she looked around through the churning haze of the dust. Had she made some terrible mistake? Had she somehow shattered and ruined the spell?

But as she stood helpless in the middle of the room, she heard a new sound. A strange, soft rustling, like leaves in a gentle breeze. And as the rustling grew around her, it seemed to change and become, instead, the whispering of gentle voices. Girls' voices, murmuring words that chilled Garland to the marrow . . .

> *'But if the promise you should break,*
> *Another pledge the Nine shall make,*
> *And we shall come, and we shall take*
> *Your life in payment, for their sake.'*

The last verse of the song . . . and the Nine

Men's dire pledge of vengeance. Silence fell again, and an icy sensation clutched at Garland's spine as she realized what she had heard. Those rustling, unhuman sounds were the voices of the Nine Men's lost consorts. Across centuries of time, the Nine Ladies had spoken to her and given her warning.

Garland looked around the ballroom. Everything was quiet and still now. The spinet was silent. The carved wooden pillars were motionless.

And outside in the moonlit night, Coryn was waiting for the first, dreadful sounds of the Nine Men's approach . . .

Desperation rose in Garland again. She had sung the song; she had danced the dance. The spell had begun to work – but it had only begun. It was not yet complete. Yet there seemed to be nothing more left that she could do.

'What else?' she called out, not knowing if anyone or anything could hear her. 'What else *is* there? I have tried! Oh, won't you tell me what you want?'

A little breath of wind blew through the ballroom. It came from nowhere, ruffling Garland's hair as it passed. It sighed, and in the sigh Garland thought she heard a disembodied echo that sounded almost like words:

THE FEEEEE . . . THE FEEEEE . . .

Something seemed to catch at Garland's arm,

startling her. When she looked down, she saw that her hand had moved of its own accord. Moved to the pocket of her riding coat.

The fee – of course! She still had the nine slivers of wood she had cut from the pillars, the offering which the Nine Men had ignored. Now, she must offer them again.

Garland drew the slivers from her pocket, counting them carefully into her palm. Seven . . . eight . . . nine. As she took the ninth sliver in her hand, the haunting music came shimmering back, and with it the same strange, soft voices singing in harmony as they began the old spell-song once more.

> '*Dance the dance and step the measure,*
> *Nine for joy and nine for pleasure.*
> *Our delight shall be your treasure* –
> *Let the dance go on for ever . . .*
> *Let the dance go on for ever . . .*
> *Let the dance go on for ever . . .*'

Over and over again the voices repeated the last line of the verse, and suddenly Garland found her feet beginning to move again. Unable to stop herself, she turned, pirouetting, marking out once more the steps of the magical dance. This time, though, the dance was not a mad whirl but slow and graceful. And Garland's own voice joined with the ghostly choir as she, too, sang the line.

'Let the dance go on for ever . . . let the dance go on for ever . . .'

Without warning a wind sprang up again, and this time it hit Garland with the force of a gale. She cried out in shock, swaying and almost losing her balance; there came a vast, rushing sound that dinned in her ears, and then –

Silence. The wind vanished, everything in the ballroom was utterly still. Blinking, pushing the tangle of her hair from her eyes, Garland looked –

And froze.

The nearest of the carved pillars was changing. Its outlines seemed to writhe and shift, and a shape began to take form within it. Garland saw a lovely face, hair like leaves, a slender form . . . Now the other columns were changing too, more faces and figures appearing. Like phantoms in the moonlight, nine beautiful but unhuman girls appeared from within the pillars, and stepped into the room.

Garland's eyes widened in awe and disbelief. She opened her mouth, struggled to find words, but no words would come. All she could do was stand rigid, as though she herself were rooted like a tree, as the first of the Nine Ladies glided towards her. An exquisite face – delicate as carved white wood – smiled. Eyes as green as young leaves sparkled. And a hand supple as a branch reached out to touch Garland's hand, and to pluck one of the slivers from her palm.

Stunned, and still unable to move, Garland stayed motionless as, one by one, the Nine Ladies filed past her, each taking one of the wood slivers from her grasp. Oak, elm, aspen . . . they were all here. They had returned. And the fee which for so long had set a curse on Coryn's family had at last been paid once more!

Finally, the last wraithlike figure took the final offering. And in the same moment the thrall that had held Garland was broken. Suddenly, the fear that had had her in its grip vanished. She felt as light as air. She felt filled with life, with energy. She wanted to *dance*!

'Dance the dance and step the measure . . .' Oh, but the magic was surging again, rushing through her! 'Nine for joy and nine for pleasure . . .' Now she was singing, and the strains of music were flowing back again to accompany her. One foot began to tap in rhythm –

'Our delight shall be your treasure – let the dance go on for ever!'

And Garland was dancing, spinning like a whirlwind, as an excitement she had never known in her life flooded through her veins. The first of the Nine Ladies grasped hold of her hand; one by one the rest joined up, forming a long line that curved around the ballroom. Suddenly they were moving together, and Garland knew that this energy would be boundless and she could dance for a thousand days, a thousand miles!

She gave a singing cry of joy, and the Nine Ladies answered in glorious concert. And as the music swirled around them, Garland led her wonderful, eerie procession dancing towards the ballroom door.

CHAPTER XI

CORYN STOOD still, gazing across the moonlit garden to where the forest began. The trees looked dark and sinister, and the rustle of their leaves sounded like voices whispering to him. As if they were mocking his plight . . .

He felt numb. He had expected to be afraid, but somehow the feeling wasn't there. *Nothing* was there. All he knew was a strange, dull sense of resignation and apathy. He had accepted his destiny, and nothing mattered to him any more.

Yet in a dark corner of Coryn's heart, one small but agonizing fire still burned – the fire of his love for Garland. Twice he had spoken her name aloud, though she wasn't there to hear him, and when he thought of her it was hard to keep tears from welling in his eyes. He had seen her run indoors, and had heard no sound from inside the house since then. He was glad that she had done what he asked of her. Glad she would not have to watch him die.

The night was very quiet. Only the dismal hooting of an owl broke the silence, and after a while even that ceased. But then Coryn heard something else in the distance. Heavy and rhythmic, approaching slowly but surely, it was a sound like tramping feet.

A feeling of cold helplessness washed over Coryn, and just for a moment he thought that he might, after all, feel frightened. But the quick little spark of terror faded away again, and he only stood like a statue. Watching. Waiting.

He saw the leaves shake before the Nine Men appeared. One by one, they emerged from the forest into the moonlight: tall, gaunt figures that moved with grim purpose. They formed a half circle before Coryn, and still he did not move but could only stare, as if their power had already hypnotized him. He could see their eyes glittering like gems under their furrowed brows. He could feel the deadly, unearthly power that burned in them . . .

The Nine Men halted, and for several seconds there was utter silence as they gazed steadily, cruelly at Coryn. Then the tallest took a menacing step forward.

The stone figure did not speak. There was no movement of its mouth, no change in its expression. But in his mind Coryn heard a voice, deep and grating like something from a nightmare, and he knew that it came from the leader of the Nine Men.

The voice said: 'Do you come to dance, or do you come to die?'

Coryn's mouth and throat were dry; he licked his lips, trying to moisten them. This, his mother had told him, was the question that the Nine always asked. The question to which there was no longer an answer. Haltingly, he answered aloud, 'I would rather dance than die. But –'

He was not allowed to finish; the eerie voice spoke in his head once more, relentlessly. 'Do you bring the fee that must be paid?'

Coryn hung his head. 'I have brought nothing,' he whispered. 'Only myself, as the ancient pact tells me I must.'

There was a pause. The stone figures stood motionless. Then, with quiet but lethal certainty, the voice in his mind uttered its damning judgement.

'Then,' it said, 'you shall die.'

With a heavy lurching the Nine Men began to move, forming a circle around Coryn. Coryn stood his ground, not knowing what they meant to do, or what he should or could do. He felt as if he had frozen inside. He wanted to scream, to plead, but he couldn't make a sound. He was completely powerless. Like a mouse mesmerized by a cat, he could only watch as the nine figures gathered around him. Then, slowly, they began to close in. And for the first time Coryn realized how he would die. They were crowding in on him, shrinking the circle around him. And they intended to press tighter, tighter, until finally they crushed him between their unyielding stone forms.

Suddenly, the terror that had been beyond

Coryn broke through. He felt it rise in him, felt the panic of despair, and his voice broke from his throat in a gasp. 'No – ah, no!' He flung his hands up, trying to ward them off. But his fingers touched immovable stone, and he knew that mere human strength could never be enough to stand against the power of the Nine Men. He was going to die. He was going to –

'No!'

The cry came from the direction of the house. The Nine Men stopped in their tracks, and with a gasp of shock Coryn swung round.

Through a gap in the stone figures crowding round him he saw Garland framed in the doorway. Her hair was awry and her cheeks flushed with excitement. And her expression was radiant.

'No!' she cried again. 'Wait – you must not strike!' She flung out one arm towards the hall behind her. 'I have brought the fee!'

Suddenly, from within the house, came the strains of music. And an instant later, a chorus of sweet voices started to sing.

'*Dance the dance and step the measure,*
Nine for joy and nine for pleasure . . .'

As the song rose into the night air, Garland began to dance. She moved from the doorway and into the garden, and Coryn's eyes widened in amazement as, behind her, he saw nine lovely, ethereal shapes emerging from the house. Hand in hand, with Garland leading them, the Nine Ladies came dancing across the grass. The stone warriors turned and saw them. They drew back a little way from Coryn . . .

The graceful procession reached the crushing circle, and with a flourish Garland halted before the leader of the Nine Men. 'See!' she cried exultantly. 'The pact has been fulfilled – I have brought your ladies back to you!'

At Garland's side the first of the Nine Ladies had also stopped. She smiled. She held out her arms towards the stone figure.

A strange sound, like a sigh, whispered across the garden. Though they had no true voices, the sound seemed to come from the Nine Men . . . or was it, Coryn asked himself dazedly, only his imagination, running at fever pitch? But whatever the truth, the sigh was one of satisfaction, and of approval. Slowly, very slowly, the Nine stepped back, leaving Coryn free. And, one by one, the nine beautiful wood spirits took the hands of their stone consorts. The music swelled in the air briefly, then paused on a trembling note, and gravely the leader of the Nine Men turned to gaze at the shocked Coryn. The glitter of hatred was gone from the figure's eyes, and for the last time the terrible, spectral voice spoke in his mind.

'It is well,' the voice said. 'The fee is paid, and there is no need for vengeance.' Suddenly the lines of the hard stone mouth seemed to change, and something that could almost have been a smile formed on the figure's face. The voice continued: 'Now, you and your beloved shall join our revel. For that, too, was part of the pact we made with your ancestor.'

Coryn was too stunned to answer, but Garland ran to him and caught hold of his arm. 'Coryn,' she said eagerly, 'Coryn, dance with me! Let us make merry with the Nine Men and their ladies, just as your forefathers used to do!' She swung him to face her, smiling into his bemused eyes. 'Dance, Coryn! There will be no more unhappiness for us!'

The strains of magical music swelled again, lively now, adding its own power to Garland's plea. Coryn didn't resist as she took both his hands in hers. His feet started to move. His body caught the rhythm and began to sway. A step to the left; a step to the right – and suddenly they were dancing together, over the grass, around the garden, ignoring the brambles and the briars as the spell ensnared them. Around them, the Nine Men and their consorts, too, began to whirl and sway with the music; then, urged by instinct and the magic, they all formed up into a long line. The music paused; the Nine Men bowed to their ladies, the ladies curtsied to the ground, and Coryn and Garland did the same. Then, sparkling out of the air, a new tune began, quicker and livelier – and the entire group danced away on to the forest track. In among the trees they wove, on and on, the music compelling them faster with every moment, until suddenly they burst out of the woodland and the hill was before them. Clear moonlight showered down on the scene, but there were no standing stones to cast long shadows now. For the Nine Men were dancing, and Coryn and Garland were among them, joining in their revelry as Coryn's ancestors had done so long ago.

On they went, on up the grassy slope to the hilltop. And there under the shining moon the ancient bond between the spirit world and the world of humans was renewed as the dance continued. There was no one to witness their eerie celebration, no one to hear the music's shimmering, ghostly melodies. To Garland and Coryn, caught up in each other's arms, it was as if they had stepped outside time and into another world. They were enthralled by the magic, never tiring, never flagging, and they danced as though the night would be endless. They danced, and they danced, and they danced . . .

Until, breaking through the dreamlike enchantment, Garland felt a tingle of warmth on her face. She blinked in surprise –

And opened her eyes to find herself looking at the rising sun.

Garland gave a gasp and sat up. *Sat up? But –* Shocked, she looked wildly about her. *What had happened? Where was she?*

Then her vision cleared, and she saw.

She had been lying on the soft turf at the very top of the hill, her head pillowed on a tussock of grass. Dawn had just broken, and the entire hill sparkled diamond-bright with dew. Garland's pulse began to race as she remembered all that had happened, and fear filled her. Had the incredible, mystical events of the night been nothing more than a dream? Had she imagined it all, and was Coryn still in peril? Or – and suddenly, horribly, her heart seemed to stop beating altogether – had the worst already happened? Had the Nine Men taken their revenge, and was Coryn now lying dead in the tangled garden of his home?

Garland cried out then, a cry of grief and terror, and started to scramble to her feet.

And a voice, drowsily surprised, said, 'Garland . . .?'

She spun round. Ten paces away, Coryn was sitting up and rubbing at his eyes. For several seconds they stared at each other. Then Garland flew across the grass and hurled herself into Coryn's arms.

'Oh, Coryn, Coryn!' She was sobbing with relief, joy and bewilderment all at once. 'I thought – I feared . . .'

He gripped her shoulders, his blue eyes intense. 'Garland, we were dancing!' he said. 'Dancing with the Nine Men and their ladies, and the pact was fulfilled!' He paused, and fear crept into his look. 'Was it a dream?'

Garland shook her head. 'I don't know. But if it was, then I dreamed it, too.'

Uneasily, they looked around them. Only moments ago, or so it seemed, the hill had been alive with music and merriment. Now, there was nothing to be seen.

Nothing but nine tall stones, forming a circle on the hilltop.

Taking a tight hold of Garland's hand, Coryn moved towards the nearest of the stones. Reaching it, he stopped and stared hard, seeking some trace of a face, a figure, in its rough surface. But there was no trace. It was lifeless granite, nothing more.

Suddenly Garland glimpsed something in the grass at the foot of the stone. She bent quickly to pick it up. Then, without a word, she held it out to Coryn.

It was a sliver of wood. And when they walked slowly around the circle, they found eight more slivers, each one lying by a standing stone.

Gently Garland and Coryn put the wood slivers back in their places, then for a long time they stood in silence, gazing at each other. There was no need for words, for there could be no doubt of the truth now. Last night had not been a dream. It had been real. The Nine Men had returned to claim their fee, and for the first time in many generations that fee had been paid. The old, lost secret of the pact had been rediscovered, and the curse on Coryn's family was broken at last.

The sun was climbing in the sky, warming them. Coryn raised his hands, cupped Garland's face between his fingers, then leaned forward and kissed her. It was a kiss of love, and of a gratitude which he would never be able to find the words to express. Then, as their lips finally parted, he said,

'Will they believe us? Your parents, and my mother? Will they ever believe what happened to us last night?'

A small frown came to Garland's face as she remembered the part their parents had all played in this ... and their selfish motives in keeping the deadly secret of the standing stones. But then she thought: *What does it matter? They were the cowards. We were not – we succeeded, where they had only failed!*

The cloud melted from her mind and she laughed. 'Seeing is believing! And we are here to prove the truth to them and to everyone!'

Coryn laughed, and the hill and the forest echoed the sound back exuberantly. Then, suddenly serious, he touched Garland's face again.

'When we are married, Garland, there will be no sorrow in our home. Only happiness.'

She smiled tremulously, her heart aching with joy. 'And music,' she added softly.

Coryn smiled too. 'And dancing.'

Garland thought of the neglected ballroom. It

must have been so beautiful in the past. In time, they could make it beautiful again. And in years to come it would be the setting for the grandest revels the district had ever seen. That would be their special tribute. A tribute to Nine Men and Nine Ladies . . .

'Oh, yes.' She held his hands and, playfully, raised them up, as though waiting for music to begin. 'Always, *always* dancing.'

About the Author

Louise Cooper was born in Hertfordshire in 1952. She hated school so much – spending most lessons clandestinely writing stories – that she persuaded her parents to let her abandon her education at the age of fifteen, and has never regretted it. Her first novel was published when she was twenty; moving to London in 1975, she worked in publishing before becoming a full-time writer in 1977. Since then she has published more than twenty fantasy novels, in both the adult and children's fields, and has ideas for many more to come. She also writes occasional short stories, and poetry for her own pleasure.

Also in the DARK ENCHANTMENT series

The Shrouded Mirror
by LOUISE COOPER

CHAPTER I

A S THE CARRIAGE pulled up in the courtyard of the great house, Aline's stomach
felt as if it was full of butterflies. She
heard the coachman get down, and moments
later the carriage door was opened. She stepped
out, and saw her new home for the very first time.

The house looked daunting. High, grey stone
walls towered before her to a roof of gables and
tall chimneys, and wide, stone steps led up to an
imposing front door. Aline clutched her small
valise more tightly and tried not to tremble.

She could hardly believe that she was here.
Everything had happened so *quickly*. Only a
week ago she had been working as a humble
helper at the dreary little school in her home
village. Then Mrs Rosell had come into her life,
and everything had changed.

Mrs Rosell was the housekeeper at a mansion a day's drive away from Aline's village. Her employer, a young man whom she referred to as 'Master Orlando', had asked her to find a girl to become a companion to his sister, who had been injured in an accident and could no longer walk. Someone in the village had recommended Aline, and so Mrs Rosell had come to the school to see her. And to Aline's astonishment, she had offered her the post on the spot.

Aline's parents had been delighted, for this was an undreamed-of chance for their daughter. From a lady's companion, Aline might move on to become a proper teacher one day, or even a governess. It was a step up in the world. And so, hardly knowing what to think or what to do, Aline had accepted Mrs Rosell's offer.

Now, though, she felt desperately nervous. What awaited her here? Would she like her new employers and, more importantly, would they like her? And could she, a girl from a poor home, settle happily into life among wealthy strangers?

As the thoughts churned in her mind the front door opened and Mrs Rosell came out. She was a small, plump, comfortable-looking woman, and she greeted Aline with a smile.

'Here you are, my dear! Come in, come in. I'll take you to your room. Hurry, now – Miss Orielle is anxious to meet you.'

Heart thumping and feeling queasy, Aline followed her up the steps and into the entrance hall. She had a bewildering impression of fine tapestries, polished floors and several huge and shining gilt-framed mirrors before Mrs Rosell led her up a wide, sweeping staircase to the upper floor. Then came the maze of corridors, richly carpeted and with more mirrors on the walls, until at last a door was opened and she was shown into the room that would be hers from now on.

Aline stood on the threshold and stared. The room was *huge*, and beautifully furnished with a fine bed, elegant dressing-table and thick rugs on the floor.

'I've never seen such a lovely room,' she said wonderingly. 'Is it really for me?'

Mrs Rosell smiled. 'All for you, child. It's next door to Miss Orielle's bedroom, so you'll be close by if she needs anything at night.'

Aline went to the window – her feet made no sound on the plush rugs – and looked out. The window gave a view of elegant gardens, with hedges, statues and paved paths meandering between beds filled with spring flowers. To the left was a high hedge with parkland beyond, and to the right –

Aline was suddenly motionless as she saw what lay to the right. Another part of the house ... but it was a ruin. The windows had no glass, and half the roof had fallen in, leaving rafters gaping starkly to the sky. She could see a huge hole where a chimney-stack had once stood. And the stonework was blackened, as if it had been burned.

'Ah ... the old north wing.' Mrs Rosell had moved up so quietly that Aline jumped. Aline looked at her, and saw that her eyes were filled with sadness – and also with a hint of bitter anger.

'There was a fire?' she asked softly.

'Yes,' said Mrs Rosell. 'It happened two years ago. The blaze started in the middle of the night. The whole family slept in that wing then, and by the time the alarm was raised, the fire had too great a hold.' She sighed. 'Master Orlando was so brave. He got Miss Orielle to safety. But the poor master and mistress ... no one could reach them in time.'

Aline's eyes widened. She had been told that her employers' parents were both dead, but she hadn't dreamed that it had happened in such a terrible way. She said so, and Mrs Rosell replied sombrely, 'Well, now you know the story. And since that night, Miss Orielle has been unable to walk.'

'She was hurt?' Aline asked.

But to her surprise, Mrs Rosell shook her head. 'Not seriously. She was trapped when a beam fell, but by a miracle she suffered no real physical harm. It was the shock of it, that was what the doctors said. They believe she *could* walk again, if only she could find the will. But somehow she can't bring herself even to try.' A sad smile came to her face and she met Aline's gaze. 'Now that you're here, though, who knows that that might not change? Perhaps all she needs is a friend to help her. That's what Master Orlando hopes.'

Aline felt a prickle of discomfort. Whatever sort of person, she wondered, was Master Orlando expecting her to be? If he thought that she might succeed where all the doctors had failed, then she would surely disappoint him. She was no miracle-worker. She was nothing special at all.

Mrs Rosell, oblivious of Aline's uneasiness, said briskly, 'Now, my dear, you'd better get ready and come downstairs. Tea will be ready in the drawing-room, and Miss Orielle is waiting.'

Aline's nerves gave a sharp little tingle and, mouth dry, she nodded.

'Oh, and one last thing,' added Mrs Rosell. 'Whatever you do, don't mention Miss Orielle's accident in her hearing. Or the fire.' She sighed. 'She and Master Orlando don't like to be reminded of it. That's very important, and you mustn't ever forget.'

'I understand,' Aline said. 'I'll be careful.'

Mrs Rosell gave her directions to the drawing-room, then left her to prepare herself. When she had gone, Aline changed her travelling clothes for a plain but respectable day dress – the best one she had – then sat down before the dressing-table mirror to tidy her hair. Her face, gazing back at her from the glass, looked pinched and a little frightened, and with a great effort she made herself smile and relax. That was better: at least she looked more confident, even if she didn't feel it. After all, she told herself, she had nothing to be afraid of.

She began to brush her hair. It was the colour of corn and, her mother always said, the only thing that prevented her from being plain. Behind her she could see the reflection of the window with its long curtain. Then, as the brush smoothed rhythmically down, the curtain stirred suddenly.

Aline started and swung round. Odd ... the window wasn't open and there was no draught. And the curtain was motionless now. That glimpse in the mirror must have been her imagination. Silly of her.

With a small shrug, she turned to the glass again and continued with her brushing.

'Miss Orielle,' said Mrs Rosell, 'here is Aline.'

Aline stepped into the elegant drawing-room. In its centre was a big, highly polished table, where fine china and silver were set out ready for tea. Beyond the table were tall windows that let in the afternoon sun. And by one of the windows, someone was sitting in a wheeled chair.

Small white hands reached out and expertly

turned the chair around, and Orielle said. 'Aline – welcome to our house.'

Orielle was about the same age as Aline. And she was beautiful, with jet-black hair, porcelain skin and grey eyes that had real warmth in them. There was warmth in her smile, too, and Aline's nerves melted as she went forward to greet her.

'I've so looked forward to your coming,' Orielle said. 'I do hope we'll be the best of friends.'

'I hope so, too,' Aline replied with a smile. 'And ... thank you for offering me this post.'

'Thank my brother, not me,' Orielle said. 'He made all the arrangements – you'll meet him soon. Mrs Rosell, will you tell Orlando that tea is ready, please?'

'Of course, miss.' Mrs Rosell bustled out, and Orielle wheeled her chair up to the table.

'Come and sit beside me, Aline. You must be hungry after your long journey – if Orlando isn't here in five minutes, we'll start without him.'

Aline looked at the lavish spread. She had never seen anything like it, and suddenly she grew nervous again. Would her manners be good enough for such an elegant household? And as for the china ... the thought of using such beautiful cups and plates daunted her. What if nervousness made her clumsy and she broke something?

Orielle had begun to talk about the things she wanted to do now that she had a companion. Suddenly the door opened. Aline looked up and saw Orlando for the first time.

He was several years older than his sister. And if Orielle was beautiful, he was without any doubt the most handsome young man Aline had ever set eyes on. His hair, like Orielle's, was as black as ebony; he was tall, slim, and in his finely cut breeches and coat he looked the perfect model of a noble and wealthy young gentleman. And the smile on his lips and in his grey eyes made Aline's heart turn over.

'You must be Aline.' He came forward and clasped her hand in greeting. 'I'm so glad to meet you – and so glad you were able to accept the post!'

Aline hardly knew what she was saying as she stammered out a reply. She knew she was blushing deeply, but Orlando didn't seem to notice. He went to Orielle's chair and gave her a hug which she returned with an affectionate kiss. He then took his seat at the table. Orielle was eager to know all that he had been doing that afternoon, and he launched immediately into an account. It was obvious to Aline that he and his sister were very close; far closer than she and her own brothers had ever been. Somehow that reassured her, and gradually she began to recover from her initial confusion. A servant came in with tea, and as the meal progressed she slowly found the confidence to join in the cheerful talk. But she could hardly take her eyes off Orlando. And by the time they had finished eating, her confusion had taken a new turn. She not only found Orlando extremely attractive; she also truly *liked* him. And she had the impression that he liked her, or he behaved towards her with a real warmth that seemed just a little greater than mere kindness. He drew her into the conversation, wanted to know about her life and her interests, and once or twice she had caught him looking at her in a strangely thoughtful way. When he saw that she had noticed, he turned his attention back to his meal – but not before giving her a quick, encouraging smile that made her cheeks colour again.

Orielle, however, seemed unaware of Aline's fascination with her brother, and when the dishes had been cleared away she asked to be taken upstairs so that she could show Aline her bedroom. Two servants carried her in her wheelchair, and over her shoulder Orielle joked with Aline, still below in the hall, about the comical sight she must present.

'She's so cheerful,' Aline said softly to Orlando, who had come to stand beside her. 'And yet to be unable to walk ... it must be very hard for her.'

Orlando smiled a little sadly. 'I think she's grown used to it now.'

'Mrs Rosell said ...' Aline hesitated, then

decided that there was no harm in continuing. 'She said the doctors think there's no real reason why she shouldn't be able to walk.'

'That's true. Her legs are undamaged; in fact she can stand up, if she has something to hold on to. But she can't seem to make herself take that first, vital step.' Orlando looked at Aline, a strange, intense look. 'Perhaps you can help her, Aline. Perhaps you'll be able to give her the confidence she needs. I do hope so.'

Aline didn't answer. If Orlando was looking for a miracle-worker, she thought, then he had made a poor choice. She was no such thing. But she would try. For Orielle's sake – and for his.

'Aline!' Orielle's voice floated down the stairs. 'Come up and see my room!'

Orlando laughed. 'She won't be content until she's shown you all her clothes and had you try half of them on! Goodnight, Aline.' He smiled again, and although she knew it was silly of her, Aline felt an inward glow of pleasure. 'I'll look forward to seeing you tomorrow.'